THE WOVEN THREAD

THE WOVEN THREAD

Jennifer Winfield goes to work as a residential secretary at the Manor House, where Lady Barclay is researching a book of family history. Jenny intends the job to fill in time until her fiancé Peter returns from abroad. The unexpected arrival of Simon Barclay and Allan Howe, turn Jenny's world upside down. The attraction she feels for both men makes Jenny break her engagement off with Peter, but there is no certainty that Simon or Allan will take his place. Then, history seems to repeat itself, but with sinister undertones that threaten tragedy.

The Woven Thread

by

Claire Lorrimer

Dales Large Print Books
Long Preston, North Yorkshire,
BD23 4ND, England.

British Library Cataloguing in Publication Data.

Lorrimer, Claire
    The woven thread.

    A catalogue record of this book is
    available from the British Library

    ISBN   978-1-84262-864-5 pbk

First published in Great Britain in 1971 by
Hurst & Blackett Ltd., under the title *The Crimson Tapestry*
and pseudonym Patricia Robins.

Cover illustration © Susan Fox by arrangement with
Arcangel Images

The moral right of the author has been asserted

Published in Large Print 2011 by arrangement with
Claire Lorrimer

Dales Large Print is an imprint of Library Magna Books Ltd.

Printed and bound in Great Britain by
T.J. (International) Ltd., Cornwall, PL28 8RW

1

'You must be the Old Trout's new dogsbody!'

I looked up into the most compelling pair of eyes I had ever seen. Green? Or hazel? It was difficult to decide, but there was no difficulty in reading the mocking glint in them. I bristled. Although I often thought of Lady Barclay as 'the old girl', for me it was a term of affection. Simon Barclay's choice of description of my employer was vaguely disparaging.

He laughed at my expression of disapproval, his thin brown face suddenly outrageously attractive. So was his voice as he said impudently:

'Come off it, sweetie! You know very well she's as crazy as a coot. You must be too, choosing a job like this.'

'I'm very fond of Lady Barclay and I like the job very much.' I hoped the remark came out as stiffly as I meant it to, but his smile was infectious and I was in danger of catching that infection.

The young man perched himself on the edge of my desk and favoured me with a long stare of appraisal.

'Mother told me Lady B. had a new secretary but I didn't imagine anyone like you. Large, stout, with a grey bun and spectacles, I thought. I've been wasting my time! I...'

'And now you are wasting mine,' I interrupted, furious to feel myself blushing to the roots of my hair. I put out my hand to snatch back the manuscript he had picked up, but he held it out of my reach and still laughing, began to read it aloud.

'"...did on this Eleventh Day of January in the Year of our Lord Eighteen Hundred and Four attend at the Guildhall in Chichester the trial of his young friend William Blake, poet, falsely accused of uttering Seditious and Treasonable remarks such as 'Damn the King, damn all his Subjects'. William did magnificently deny such Falsehoods even as the Soldiers were uttering their Evidence and, quite rightly, he was shortly acquitted. Our mutual Friend, William Haley, was in attendance, despite his recent accident, to swear to Blake's good character. It was indeed a Proud Moment when in defiance of all Decency, the Spectators cheered his

Verdict. After the acquittal I did accompany my two poets to sup at Mrs Poole's in Mid Lavant...'"

Ridicule threaded through Simon Barclay's voice, but it was a pleasant voice to listen to and as he came to the end of the page I realised I had been more intent on that than on what he was reading.

'What's all that meant to be?' he asked without real interest, but, I suspected, just to see if I knew.

'It's a letter from Sir Frederic Barclay to his father. He was a patron of art and literature and the poets Haley and Blake were friends of his. But you must know all that...'

'I don't and don't want to know anything about any of the Barclay lot.'

Simon's voice was suddenly curt and I could have kicked myself for not remembering in time that he was, in fact, a Barclay by adoption only. None of the fascinating people in Lady Barclay's book were blood relatives of his.

But I need not have worried. He was back to teasing good humour with bewildering swiftness.

He stood up and stretched his long length with easy grace. I was used to big men.

Peter, my fiancé, was nearly six feet tall, but Simon must have topped that by several inches and he loomed high over me as he grinned and said:

'Come and have a drink. You must need one after typing out all that tripe.'

I didn't want a drink, but quite suddenly I did want to be in the company of young people again. For a whole month I had spoken to no one but my elderly employer, and much as I liked her, it would be a relief to be with my own age group if only for a short while. Even so, I hesitated, but Simon gave me no time. He took my arm and said persuasively:

'Come on. There's no need to be bashful. I'm told drinking with me is an elevating experience and one no girl should miss!'

I still hesitated. Although Simon himself had issued the invitation, I was not at all sure how his mother would receive my appearance. Lady Barclay's description of her screamed, 'Snob, snob!' She might regard a secretary as a glorified servant and have strong views on such an addition to her party.

Simon was getting impatient, pulling me none too gently towards the door and laughing at my reluctance.

'I absolutely insist that you come with me,' he said. 'But first tell me your name. I can't dangle you on one hand, wave the other airily and say, "Mother, this is 'er".'

'It's Jenny,' I said, and laughed. It was impossible not to in the face of his absurdities.

'Jenny?' he repeated. 'Very oldy-worldy for a modern miss. I shall call you Jennifer.'

It was a silly thing to be pleased about, but I was. Peter never called me Jennifer and to have a new name was like starting a new chapter to a book.

Although I liked Simon well enough, I can't say I liked his friends. They were an odd collection. Most of the girls had high-pitched 'society' voices and seemed incapable of using them in anything but an inane babble of senseless chatter. And the men were not much better – Hooray Henry types. All of them seemed pretty tight to me, though I couldn't see much drink circulating.

Julia Barclay appeared only briefly and was much as I imagined she would be: brittle, hard, smartly dressed and made up so cleverly that she looked very little older than her son and his friends. She weighed me up with a long stare when Simon introduced me, and I stared back, waiting for the snub I felt sure would come. To my surprise she made an obvious effort to be pleasant.

'You must join in all the young people's fun,' she said. 'Life must be very boring stuck down here alone with my poor old mother-in-law.'

I was about to deny I was bored, but she had lost interest in me already. She turned her full attention on Simon. To me it was obvious she genuinely adored her son. In fact, her manner toward him was more like a lover than a mother. She almost flirted with him and Simon seemed to like it. He patted her hand affectionately and said:

'What about a little drink for you, Ma?'

She shook her head as she moved off to greet a middle-aged man who had just entered the room. Simon scowled.

'God! I might have guessed *he'd* be here. That, dear Jennifer, is Jason Macclesfield, author, and Ma's current passion.'

He seemed to see nothing unusual in his candid remark, but I admit I was slightly shocked. With my suburban background 'aristocracy' had never had the chance to become more than a romantic idea. It was disconcerting to discover a real 'Lady' could behave in a way that, to my mind, was anything but aristocratic. I felt better when I remembered Julia had married a title and had not been born with one. Delving into Lady Barclay's family history had bolstered my illusions and there was satisfaction in the thought that I could keep them.

I took the first opportunity to slip out of the room. The brief party had proved highly disappointing. I didn't 'fit' with Simon's friends and although he rather intrigued me I wouldn't care if I never saw the rest of the party again.

I kept well out of their way that day, spending the time typing out a chapter of old Lady Barclay's book. According to her, Charles II, while trying to escape, had travelled from Hampshire into Sussex in 1651 and had been hidden by one of her ancestors, called Percy, in a charcoal-burner's hut in the nearby forest. Poor Percy was later shot by a Cromwellian soldier on Duncton Beacon.

I had been so wrapped up in the story that the dinner gong came as a surprise and when I joined Lady Barclay in her wing of the house it was almost a shock to find her in the ankle-length old black velvet dress which was her usual evening get-up. Buried deep in the past for hours, I would have been far less surprised to see her in the elaborate garments worn by her female ancestors. There were plenty of examples of them hung about the walls of the Manor.

The Polish couple who looked after us when we were alone were quite incapable of dealing with an influx of guests and a catering firm had been called in. Old Lady Barclay and I stuffed like starving school-girls on the food sent up to us – a distinct improvement on our usual simple fare.

She glanced at me sharply as I sat down opposite her. I must have been looking a bit faraway and vague, for she smiled at me and through a mouthful of salmon mayonnaise said:

'I can see you are beginning to feel the pull of the past, my dear.'

I nodded, returning her smile. When I took on the job of resident secretary, to type the book Lady Barclay was writing about her family, I think I had expected a boring series of lavender and old lace memoirs; boring to me because I was interested in history rather than in historical romance. She never did tell me her age, but I knew she was well over seventy and I couldn't have been more wrong in my first impression of this frail, vague old lady! She might seem almost senily absentminded about everyday affairs, but the research she had put into her family's past was an astonishing accomplishment. Drawing on old documents, reference books, memoirs, old letters and anything else she could lay her hand on, she had compiled a fascinating account of her family from the time of the siege of Arundel Castle in 1102.

'It has taken me a lifetime to gather the facts for this book,' she had told me at our mutual interview a month ago. 'Now, with your help, my dear, I am ready to write it.'

Any doubts I may have had about taking on the job for a whole year evaporated then and there. The old lady's almost obsessional enthusiasm for the task was infectious and she discussed it with none of the rambling, flowery phrases she had used when writing to tell me more about the job she advertised. I must admit her letter had depressed me and I was in anything but a hopeful frame of mind when I went for the interview.

Because of my ruined wedding plans and what I believed to be my broken heart, my one idea was to get as far away as possible from London, with all its memories of Peter, the man I should have married this very June. With the wedding date fixed, the mortgage on a country cottage signed and sealed, Peter had suddenly decided to take a two-year appointment abroad. I had given in my notice to the firm where I worked and was too proud to ask them to take me back. In any case, they had filled my job already.

If Peter had chosen a country where I could go too, it would not have mattered. But the job he wanted was strictly for a bachelor and nothing I said could change his mind about applying for it. I fancy the big money was the attraction, although he said the engineering experience would be of enormous value in the future and that was what he was after. He took the view that I was unreasonable to make such a fuss over the two-year postponement of our wedding.

I tried to believe I was being selfish, but I did not convince myself. It boiled down to Peter preferring material advantage to marriage with me. We had a flaming row which nearly ended in a broken engagement, but I was too much in love to let him go away nursing a rage against me. I swallowed my pride, apologised humbly and went to Heathrow to see him off. Tall, with serious blue eyes and a too determined chin, Peter went through passport control and waved himself out of my life. He was twenty-five, the age I would be when he came home again. Dry-eyed, I watched him go, knowing that I could never have left him and still completely unconvinced that it was right to put a career before love.

The cottage we were buying was a dream. Built of Sussex stone with a tiled roof and smothered in wisteria and roses, it was the answer to any calendar painter's prayer. Both Peter and I had long ago determined to live in the country when we were married. Here, between Chichester and Midhurst, it would have been easy enough to commute to London. The cottage had seemed ideal and now I was faced with the dismal task of letting it, instead of moving in as Peter's wife.

The local paper seemed the obvious place to look for tenants, so I bought one at the station on my way to see the estate agents. It was while I was travelling back to London with nothing to read but the paper that I saw Lady Barclay's advertisement. On the spur of the moment I decided to apply for the job and as soon as I arrived back at my dreary bedsitter I wrote to her. Her reply was so vague I doubt if I would have followed it up if the estate agents had not telephoned asking me to go down and point out what fittings and furniture I would be taking away from the cottage. I hated the idea of strangers using the stuff Peter and I had bought for ourselves, but it did seem silly to start removing things if it could be avoided. I went down to see the agents and since the cottage was at the bottom of Lady Barclay's drive I decided I might as well call on her at the same time. We took to each other at first sight and I moved into the Manor a week later.

Until now our solitude had been un-broken. I had yet to meet Lady Barclay's brother, a man in his sixties, who spent most of the year in London. His passion in life was politics and he haunted the House of Lords. Lady Barclay said it was his refuge as well as his occupation. He had lost his first wife in a riding accident, and not long after his only child, Charles, the son and heir, in a ghastly fire in the east wing of the Manor. Lord Barclay had become a recluse until some years later, when to everyone's surprise he married an old school friend of his dead wife's and adopted her son by her first marriage. Simon was now twenty-four; 'handsome and weak', was how Lady Barclay described him. For some reason she did not like talking about him, but of her little nephew Charles, who had died in the fire, she spoke often and lovingly. The little boy would, I knew, feature at the end of her book, for he was the last of the Barclay family – unless, of course, Julia produced another heir and that seemed unlikely.

Lady Barclay was a little acid in her description of Julia. She made her sound a hard, ambitious, self-indulgent society type who had married for money and title. If there had been any love between the elderly Lord Barclay and his forty-eight-year-old wife my employer made it plain there was none left now. Lady Barclay said she kept firmly to her own private rooms when Julia came down to the Manor for one of her weekend parties. She grinned wickedly as she added that Julia considered her senile and that she encouraged this opinion since it was a good excuse to keep away from the bickering that went on between the couple.

I felt curiously happy that evening. After Peter's departure I had expected to feel near suicidal. My parents were dead, so I had no one else but Peter to love. I had loved him for four years, devoting every moment of my spare time to him. Suddenly and almost without warning I was alone with time to think, to act without consideration for anyone but myself.

I thought to live each day as it came. But there were seven hundred days to be lived through before Peter returned and I found that even without him there was a lot I could enjoy. I went for long walks in the forest adjoining the Manor, taking Lady Barclay's smelly but lovable old spaniel, Bramble, with me. The trees were lovely and all at the height of their glorious spring green. There were mild adventures, too. At any turn in the forest paths I could meet badgers, pheasants, hares, weasels – wild life I had not seen since my childhood.

I missed Peter and at times longed passionately for him, but in an odd way I was becoming detached – a lack of emotion I would not have believed possible a month ago. It wasn't that I had stopped loving him, but I was discovering he wasn't quite as indispensable as I had imagined. What with my deep interest in the Barclay family history, my work indoors and my explorations out of doors, these happy interludes were occurring surprisingly often.

Lady Barclay was still staring at me over the dinner table. She had a habit of doing this and was not in the least disconcerted when I caught her at it. Now, as usual, she smiled. I was growing quite fond of her and despite the vast gap of years between us, we were fast becoming friends; friendly enough for me to ask her why she peered at me so often. She hedged a little.

'Why not, my dear child? You are very pretty – beautiful brown eyes and a lovely mouth. I like pretty things.'

With deliberate cunning she made me laugh, but it did not stop me prodding her.

'You must have a better reason than just to admire my charms!' I said. 'Why the careful and so frequent study?'

Her faded blue eyes took on a faraway look – as they did when she was at work on her book.

'It is just … just that you remind me of someone,' she said slowly. 'Jenny, do you believe in reincarnation?'

'Being reborn into another life, you mean? I don't know. I've never thought about it, but I suppose it is possible,' I said tactfully.

'I'm sure it happens.' The old lady spoke with a conviction she usually reserved for the past. 'And you, Jenny, I am quite certain, lived in this very house, many years ago. Have you ever thought that something more than pure chance brought you here?'

I didn't want to squash her romantic ideas, but I could not help grinning. She did not seem to mind.

'After dinner,' she said, 'I will show you a description of one of my ancestors, Edwina. In 1742 she married the then Lord Barclay's eldest son, John, when she was only fourteen, and she had six children by him.'

'That doesn't sound like me!' I said. But I had to admit that the description of Edwina could have applied to me. I was curious enough to ask if there was a portrait of her.

Lady Barclay shook her head regretfully.

'I am sure there was one because I found a reference to it in an article printed in 1792. It said "the hanging in chains of a robber by the name of Thomas Ellmann who, whilst in the employ of Sir John Barclay did in spite destroy the Portrait of His Lordship's Lady Edwina". The servant declared he had been dismissed unfairly and "wrought what evil he could within the house" before he was caught.'

'And wasn't Edwina ever painted again?' I was still curious.

'She died a year later. Unless an earlier painting turns up we shall never know what she really looked like.'

I wrote to Peter that night and told him the story, partly to fill in space and partly to show him how steeped in the past my old girl was and how even I was beginning to get involved in the book I was helping to write.

Peter's letters to me were far from frequent. There had been only three in the month he had been gone. I made feeble excuses for him, telling myself that like most men, he hated writing letters, that he was busy settling into his new job, and probably had more outside interests than I could find at Barclay Manor. But that did not stop me glooming in bed before I fell asleep. I had a nasty fear, mixed with resentment, that Peter's love for me wasn't as deep as I had once imagined it to be. His letters were affectionate enough but I couldn't find that note of intense longing that steeped into mine when I wrote to him. I hoped child-ishly that he would not miss the intended dig in the reference to Edwina. I had made a point of telling him she had been married at fourteen and had had six children by the time she was my age. I could guess what his reply would be – a caustic *'No doubt Lord Barclay could afford them!'*

Perhaps, I thought wryly, I would have done better to have written about Simon Barclay instead of Edwina. Peter might con-ceivably feel a spark of jealousy if I'd given a

25

rapturous description of Simon's physical attractions which I could have done quite truthfully, and, more important, Simon's attentions to me. I looked at the letter propped on my bedside table ready for posting in the morning, but I was too sleepy to be bothered to alter it and in the morning I forgot.

I had only just finished breakfast when Simon drifted into the room with an invitation to join the party about to leave for a day at the horse trials.

'I couldn't even if I wanted to,' I told him. 'I'm a working girl!'

'Oh, no you're not, sweetie. I've seen the Old Trout and she says you're welcome to a day off as you're up to date with the typing and she's busy on a new chapter or something.'

I was speechless for a moment. Whatever else, this young man was resourceful. My ego, at a fairly low ebb thanks to Peter, took a step upwards. All the same, I had no intention of becoming involved with the group I'd met yesterday. They weren't my type.

'I haven't the slightest interest in horses,' I told him truthfully, 'but thanks for asking me.'

He leaned against the breakfast table and

smiled down at me.

'Neither have I,' he said. 'We'll give the others a miss and go to the seaside. I've always wanted to know "What the butler saw"!'

It was impossible not to laugh and suddenly I wanted to go. I wanted to do something young and silly, like putting pennies into slot machines with an attractive young man who found me attractive. I'd been staid for too long. A day out would be good, not only for my morale, but for my mind.

I couldn't have had a more perfect companion in my present mood – or was it Simon who evoked the mood in the first place? We drove down to Brighton in his Aston Martin, breaking all speed limits on the way, and whisked from the pier to the Chamber of Horrors to the Aquarium where the dolphins were performing their party piece. We subsided exhausted over lunch in a pub on the Downs.

It was fun – simple, easy fun and I was happy in a carefree way that made me feel about twelve years old. It wasn't until the afternoon was over – spent as childishly as the morning had been – and we were driving home that Simon made me realise that he, at least, was not in a twelve-year-old frame of mind. His conversation became suddenly serious – and personal.

'You're good fun, Jennifer,' he said. 'We hit it off together, don't we? Let's not break up the party. Let's make a night of it.'

There was no mistaking his meaning. I suppose I should have had sense enough to guess this sort of suggestion would crop up sooner or later, but I was sorry it had. I wasn't by any means a prude but I didn't go along with the total permissiveness of the types Simon mixed with – if the crowd he brought home was anything to go by. I sighed. Somehow it spoiled the day.

'Sorry!' I said briefly. 'Perhaps you didn't know I am engaged.'

To my surprise, Simon laughed.

'I know all about you, beautiful. But, unless my spies are sadly wrong, the fiancé is a conveniently long way off. You like me, don't you?'

I was determined there should be no mis-understanding and spoke as bluntly as he had.

'I think you are extremely attractive and I've loved every minute of today but that's as far as it goes. Sorry, Simon!'

Again he surprised me by laughing. I had expected him to argue.

'All right – if that's how you feel. There's plenty of time and I always get what I want in the end. So look out, Barclay Manor, here we come!'

He jammed his foot hard down on the accelerator and we shot forward at a speed which had me clinging speechlessly to the side of the car. I think Simon was hoping I'd beg him to slow down, but nothing on earth would have made me admit I was terrified. It was stupid of me and I blamed myself afterwards for the accident we were rushing to meet.

It all happened so suddenly I can't be clear about the details. I know only that we were going too fast. Ignoring the rule of round-abouts, Simon barely slowed and though the driver of the car coming in from the right did his best to avert it, the collision was inevitable. There was a tearing noise of metal as the two cars scraped along each other and a dead silence as they stopped.

The silence did not last long. Simon, his face a sickly yellow under his tan, began a blustering string of abuse, accusations and insults aimed at the other driver whose first reaction was dumb astonishment. Then I saw him flush and in a voice as loud and furious as Simon's he shouted: 'Now, look here, you...'

I think they would have been at each other's throats in anther two minutes if, providentially, a police patrol car had not arrived on the scene. I was still trembling when the questioning started. While Simon was giving his story the other driver came over to where I was sitting by the side of the road trying to pull myself together.

'You okay?' he asked. 'I'm real sorry. Must have been a nasty shock for you.'

'It wasn't your fault,' I blurted out impulsively.

The young man gave me a glance of faint surprise as he sat down beside me. I suppose he had expected me to lam into him as Simon had.

'Glad you agree with me,' he said laconically. The short hair-cut, the light jacket over the linen trousers and the accent all proclaimed him American.

He offered me a cigarette and, as he lit it, gave me a quick smile that completely transformed his rather ugly face and for a moment made him look like a young Cary Grant.

'My name's Allan Howe,' he said. 'And you...?'

'Jennifer Winfield!'

Again that pleasant smile. I felt my tension ease slightly. But we didn't have time to follow up the introductions. The two policemen, with a considerably calmer Simon, joined us.

'Your turn now.' Simon nodded at the American. 'Bloody nuisance, isn't it, but it can't be helped. I've admitted I was in the wrong but it doesn't seem to have registered. Aren't our policemen wonderful!'

His flippancy didn't go down too well with the law and I wished he would drop it, but he kept up a similar monologue until the senior officer asked him none too politely to keep quiet while he questioned me. I couldn't help much, except to admit we were going fast though I didn't know our exact speed. Then it was Allan Howe's turn. Simon had wandered off to inspect the damage to the cars. I remained where I was, listening to the quiet interchange of question and answer.

'Full name?'

'Allan Barclay Howe.'

'Nationality?'

'American.'

'Age?'

'Twenty-seven.'

'Address?'

'Kentfield, California.'

The questions went on and on. I stopped listening for something had forced its way into my dazed mind. The American had given his name as Allan *Barclay* Howe. Or had I imagined it? It seemed a very long-odds coincidence. I knew I was still a bit bemused and one or two minor bruises were starting to hurt now the first shock was wearing off. Yet I could have sworn he did say Barclay.

I meant to ask him later, just to satisfy my curiosity, but the chance didn't arise. We were free to leave and Simon was anxious to be off. Fortunately both cars were operational.

Allan Howe, with the good manners he had already shown, came over to say goodbye. I thought he was nice, especially when without rancour he shook Simon's hand and said he'd look forward to seeing us both again soon.

As we drove away, at a reasonable speed this time, I asked Simon what Allan Howe had meant.

Simon shrugged carelessly.

'I dunno. He's turning up at the Manor to see the Old Trout about something or other. Thinks he may have vague connections with the illustrious Barclay family. Bet they are vague, too. The way these Americans harp on family origins bores me stiff.'

'But, Simon...' I paused, remembering that earlier moment of curiosity, 'perhaps he really is a connection. You weren't there when he gave his full name to the police. It was Allan *Barclay* Howe.'

'So what? Who cares?' said Simon. 'I certainly don't.'

But I did. Without knowing why, I did.

2

Lady Barclay listened to my account of Simon's accident with interest. She heard me out and surprising me as usual with her reactions, laughed delightedly.

'It's Providence at work – I know it!' she said eagerly, her voice as excited as a girl's. 'Isn't life wonderful, Jenny?'

I smiled a little wryly.

'Hardly wonderful for Simon,' I said, settling down in front of my typewriter. 'He is almost certainly going to have his licence endorsed and he says it will be for the third time.'

'Never mind about Simon.' Lady Barclay tapped my desk impatiently with the letter she was holding. 'If he isn't allowed to drive that car of his he won't be able to come down here so often and as far as I'm concerned that will be all to the good.'

For her, perhaps, but for myself I wasn't so sure. I had enjoyed my day with Simon – until the accident. For a few short hours he had laid the ghost of Peter so thoroughly that I had forgotten to post my letter to him.

Lady Barclay must have heard my faint sigh, for she peered at me and said:

'Like him, do you? Well, take my advice and keep him at a distance. That boy is no good, Jenny. Never was.'

I have the sort of nature that instinctively lines up with the underdog and I couldn't help bursting out now.

'I think you are writing him off just because he isn't really a Barclay. It's not fair. I don't suppose it has been at all easy for him being an "outsider".'

'My dear girl,' Lady Barclay said calmly as she subsided into her usual velvet-covered winged chair near my desk. 'You don't know what you're talking about. Simon made himself an "outsider" – no one else did. My brother was a very lonely man when his first wife and little Charles died. He tried hard to take both Julia and Simon to his heart. But neither of them wanted his love – only his title and his money, and, believe me, Simon has had plenty of that. In my opinion, far too much for his own good.' She peered at me over the top of her gold-rimmed spectacles and shook her head reprovingly. 'Never judge anyone without knowing all the facts, Jenny. Because my brother is so seldom down here, I suppose you imagine he neglects his family?'

I nodded reluctantly.

'I've no right to be making personal comments, anyway,' I muttered. 'I'm sorry. Please forgive me.'

At once Lady Barclay's face softened and her voice was gentle again as she said:

'My dear, it's better you should know exactly in what you may be involving yourself. There is a bad streak in Simon. He could be dangerous.'

I think Lady Barclay would have been horrified if she had realised how her warning increased my interest in Simon. Yet I knew she was right; something deep down inside me told me so. I'd seen that dangerous side to Simon yesterday when he'd risked my life as well as his own just for the sheer hell of driving his car too fast. But his wildness answered some crying need in me … I was sick of Peter's cautious approach to life. I didn't want to wait years and years for happiness while he saved for a future we might never have. He had forever talked about 'security' and 'having something behind us' and 'planning for the future'. I'd gone along with all that until he'd put his career before our marriage. From that moment on, I'd finished with tomorrow. I wanted to enjoy today.

I made no reply. Lady Barclay seized on my silence to change the conversation and began talking about the young American, Allan Howe.

'I have a letter from him, saying he is coming to see me,' she was saying. 'Last night I went through the family tree most carefully but I cannot see what possible connection he could have with our Barclays. He hasn't given me much information – only that his grandmother was English. He says he has an old letter which he thinks might interest me. Jenny, if he *could* prove a connection, it would mean an entire new chapter for my book!'

I felt a rush of affection for this dear old lady. She was as enthusiastic as a child. I hoped that when I reached her age I would be capable of feeling as deeply about something as she did about her documentation of the past. Would anyone read her book? I couldn't see it as a best seller but I suppose it would have an historical interest. Not that the fate of the book concerned Lady Barclay. She was interested only in recording the past.

'We haven't got a title for it yet,' I reminded her, seeing the blank space on the manuscript cover lying on the desk.

'I know, and I think we ought to find one. We need a frame in which we can draw up all the loose threads to make our complete picture.'

Her words gave me an idea, for they reminded me of the tapestry she had been working on every evening for the last twelve years. I had watched her, intrigued, as with infinite care and patience, she wove stitch after stitch of brilliantly coloured silks into the canvas.

'Something old and colourful,' she murmured as much to herself as to me. 'Something traditional, Jenny – perhaps with a word like "heraldic" in it.'

'Your tapestry!' I burst out. 'The Barclay heraldry. It could even be photographed when you've finished it, for the book jacket. Don't you see, Lady Barclay? Every event, each generation you've been writing about, has been like another stitch, another pattern, until little by little the picture has built up into a whole? Even the design is right – your coat of arms with all that heavenly scarlet and gold. There's your title – *The Scarlet Tapestry!*'

The old lady's cheeks were pink with delight.

'It's a wonderful idea, Jenny,' she said. 'How clever of you, dear. But I think I shall change scarlet to crimson. It sounds more royal and all our family were Royalists. *The Crimson Tapestry*. Does that sound nice to you, Jenny?'

'Almost as beautiful as the tapestry itself,' I smiled, hugging the thought that I had contributed something quite important to the book.

We might have wasted the whole morning congratulating each other but for the arrival of Allan Howe. Unheralded, he appeared in the doorway carrying a tray with the hot chocolate usually brought to us at mid-morning.

'I ran into Simon on the front doorstep and he told me to follow my nose up the main staircase and turn right,' he explained as I relieved him of the tray and indicated a chair next to Lady Barclay. 'I seized this from the woman bringing it up to you. I hope I'm not intruding?'

I introduced him to Lady Barclay and made a move to leave the room, but she nodded towards my desk.

'I want you to take notes,' she said, 'of everything Mr Howe says to me. I'm afraid my memory is bad these days, Mr Howe, so I hope you will not object? It's important I have all the details you can give me carefully noted so I can make a thorough research.'

Allan Howe took a deep breath.

'I may be on quite the wrong tack,' he said, leaning forward with his elbows on his knees and looking anything in the world but English. His short hair still looked odd, at least in contrast to Simon's fashionable mop. For a moment I lost what he was saying as I tried to imagine the American with a similar hair style. The image I conjured up was vaguely ridiculous. Perhaps, I thought, the clothes had to be in keeping, too, for the whole to look right.

'Well, that is, as far as we know, isn't it, Jenny?'

Lady Barclay's question took me unawares

and I blushed. I felt Allan Howe's amused eyes staring at my bright pink face and knew that he knew I had not been paying attention. I went a deeper red and for a moment felt furious with him for laughing at me.

'Lady Barclay was saying that none of the Barclays emigrated.' I was grateful to him for putting me wise. 'I suppose it was only a straw in the wind but I did hope I might have been able to trace my grandmother's origins while I was in England.'

'But we mustn't give up all hope.' Lady Barclay patted his knee comfortingly. 'After all, there are still a good many blanks to be filled in. I'm disappointed, too. I am very anxious to make a *complete* history of my family, but naturally I can't trace all the bastards. You could be one of them.'

I hope I concealed my gasp. I saw Allan Howe's eyes first widen and then crinkle with laughter. Lady Barclay, blissfully unaware that she had said anything that might upset or insult her guest, went on:

'I expect you know that in the old days most English milords were expected to raise a few children out of wedlock. They could not inherit, of course, but they were educated and provided for. Unfortunately they did not always take the family name, which makes it difficult to trace them.'

'I can see that!' Allan Howe laughed as he pulled a faded dog-eared letter from his pocket. It had a red sealing-wax stamp on its outer page, no envelope. He handed it over to Lady Barclay, who read it carefully and passed it to me.

In the top right-hand corner was written: *Steam Ship America* in a neat, ornate script. The date beneath was November 8th, 1854.

Dear Harry I read,

What must your astonishment have been on your arrival home to find me gone across the Atlantic. I do not regret it for I am greatly in love with Edwin. Nor do I fear for the future as far as I am concerned but for my dear Edwin I have much anxiety. However, the step is taken and I trust Providence will watch over us.

I glanced up to find Allan Howe watching me as I read. I went on, feeling the smooth surface of the old paper like a fine parchment between my fingers.

The only person I regret leaving is yourself and that without saying goodbye. It was a hard trial, Harry, for I loved you as a Brother and I trust that in your heart you will not condemn me. Of course, Papa and Mama will condemn me and I have not written to either, nor shall I till we are settled somewhere and Edwin has established himself.

We are going first to Hamilton, Canada West, it being a cheap place and where Edwin will seek employment. I will write again as soon as we arrive there.

We have had a rough passage but have met some very jolly passengers, therefore time has not hung so heavily. We shall be at Halifax in the morning where I can post this for England.

My maid, Annie, is with me and a great comfort to me and not much extra expense.

Harry, if you should hear me, or my dear Edwin, run down by others, I shall think it a great favour if you say a good word for us. We love each other truly.

We shall be at Boston on Saturday and at Hamilton I expect on Wednesday. God bless you, Harry, and bestow a thought sometimes on your unfortunate sister,

Clarissa

'Was she your grandmother?' I asked Allan Howe. He nodded.

'Clarissa Barclay. I never knew my father. He died before I was born, but my mother told me a great deal about him and his parents, Clarissa and Edwin Howe. He was their only child and when they died in a typhoid outbreak he was brought up in an orphanage in San Francisco. My mother said Clarissa had been an English lady of aristocratic birth and had eloped to the New World with her father's head groom. The romantic angle of the story intrigued me. When my mother died I found this letter among her papers and it made me decide that if and whenever I came to England I would try and trace my grandmother's family.'

Lady Barclay had her copy of the Barclay family tree spread out on the table in front of her. Our cups of chocolate had long since grown cold. She was frowning as her thin delicate white fingers traced the lines and names.

'There was a Harry Barclay born in 1830,' she announced, 'and he had six brothers and sisters, but no mention of a Clarissa among them.'

'I expect Harry was a fairly common name in those days,' Allan Howe said, standing up with a grace surprising in so large a frame. 'Thank you, anyway, for looking, Lady Barclay, and for allowing me to take up your time.'

'My dear boy, you mustn't give up so easily,' Lady Barclay said. 'Believe me, if I had abandoned hope so quickly each time I came to a dead end I would never have started this book, let alone hope to finish it.'

She soon had Allan Howe seated again while she told him of her *magnum opus, The Crimson Tapestry*. She explained the title proudly and was sweet enough to give me the credit for it. Whether he was being polite or was genuinely interested I wasn't sure, but Allan seemed as engrossed as we were in the subject; so engrossed that the lunch gong sounded very much to our surprise. Lady Barclay insisted Allan should stay to lunch with us. We had reached the Christian names stage by then.

'It will be worth eating – all the goodies left over from the weekend!' she chuckled like a greedy child. 'You must help us to finish them up, Allan, or we shall have nothing else for the rest of the week.'

The weekend guests had departed for London, Simon with them, and the house was empty and quiet, but, for once, not lonely.

Allan talked well. He told us about his studies at the St Roche Arboretum and in particular his investigations into the old art of charcoal-burning. A chapter in Lady Barclay's book was devoted to a Royalist ancestor who had escaped from Cromwell's men by disguising himself as a charcoal-burner and I could see she was drinking up all the information Allan was giving her.

'I shall read your book the moment it is published,' Allan declared. 'In fact, I may be able to help. I have some notes that may interest you. For instance, did you know that charcoal from around here was carried by barge on the river Arun to Guildford where the gunpowder factories were? And that in the old days it was made from alder trees and now it comes from beechwood?'

They were lost in a conversation which left me out. One thing was for sure my dear old Lady Barclay and Allan had more in common with each other than I had with either of them.

I knew I was being unfair. That I was feeling 'two's company, three's a crowd' was my own fault because Allan did try to include me in the conversation. I was just being perverse in refusing to join in. Mean, too, for I knew far better than Allan Howe could that any failure to find a missing link with the Barclay family past would be an enormous disappointment for Lady Barclay. The thought that a Clarissa Barclay of whom she knew nothing had perhaps existed would be tantalising to a degree. If Allan sensed that disappointment he was doing his best to distract her and it was nice of him.

I stood up when coffee came in, intending to leave them alone to continue their talk.

'I think I'll take Bramble for a walk. He didn't get one yesterday and…'

'Have your coffee first, child!' Lady Barclay sounded surprised and I could have kicked myself for my gaucherie. 'And Allan might like to go with you. The grounds are very beautiful, Allan. It might interest you to see them.'

'But what about you?' I began, and broke off as she interrupted.

'My dear child, I need a rest after all this exciting talk. You know, Allan, Jenny frequently forgets I am old enough to need a nap in the afternoon.'

'I'm not surprised she forgets,' Allan said gallantly. 'You've the mind of a young girl, Lady Barclay. How do you remember so many facts! I guess I just won't ever have that much knowledge even if I live to be twice your age.'

'Well, my memory's going, young man. That's why I want the facts down in black and white before I die and they die with me. You'll come and see me again? I'd be very happy if you could find the time.'

'Surely!' Allan said. 'I'd make time even if I hadn't plenty of it. I've enjoyed our talk, and my lunch, so much. Thank you again.'

He's too good to be true, I told myself cynically as ten minutes later we were tramping through the beechwoods, Bramble scattering the soft earth mould in all directions as he raced to and fro. Were all Americans as well mannered and polite? From the few I'd seen in business, Allan Howe was the exception rather than the rule. He was almost too suave.

I found myself wondering why I was trying to pick holes in him. He'd done nothing at all offensive, in fact had gone out of his way to be pleasant and friendly to me and had been nice enough to pretend an eagerness to go on this walk even if he was bored stiff. I had not the slightest reason to feel antagonistic, but I did. If he noticed my curt replies to his easy flow of conversation he gave no sign of it. And then, without understanding why, I was suddenly outrageously rude to him. I said:

'Did you really believe your grandmother was one of the Barclays or were you just trying to get a foot in with the aristocracy?'

It shook him out of his polite friendliness. His face turned a dull brick red. He drew in his breath sharply, stopped in his tracks and looked straight at me.

'I suppose you have a reason for that remark. I can't think what it is and I suppose I'm a fool to care, but I do. I would like you to explain what I've said or done to justify a remark like that.'

I felt my heart give a kick of – what? Anger? Or fear? Or remorse? I wasn't sure. I said coldly:

'Are you so used to having everyone like you, then, that you feel I must be added to the collection?'

I knew I was being deliberately offensive and it was exciting in an odd way. I felt instinctively that the man beside me could be dangerous – not in the way that Simon might be dangerous, but more subtly. I had already proved he was slow to rouse, but once he lost his temper...

Without thinking I put my arms up to defend myself, only to have them grabbed as, to my complete astonishment, he pulled me against him. He held me, immovable and speechless, staring down at my furious face and blazing eyes, his own unfathomable as I stared back at him. Then he kissed me.

3

It was a long, hard, strange kiss. I fought against it, fought against the sheer simple pleasure of being kissed. It was weeks since Peter had left, weeks since I'd felt a man's arms around me, strong, possessively demanding. I'd been so lonely, so hurt, so humiliated...

I felt myself softening towards the man who held me and knew, quite suddenly, that it was Peter I was fighting, not Allan Howe. I'd wanted to hurt him because I wanted to hurt Peter. I was afraid of liking him. But I knew I could never explain all that. I was heartily ashamed of the tears in my eyes as I struggled free.

As I did so he said, very gently:

'I'm sorry, Jenny.'

His words were my undoing. The tears spilled over and I was back in his arms, sobbing like some silly two-year-old.

I could have gone on crying for hours. I was certainly enjoying it to the full, feeling Allan's hand gently stroking the hair at the back of my head, loving the feeling of his tweed jacket rough against my cheek. But Bramble, interested in this strange sight, was jumping up at my legs, laddering my tights. Allan released me, offering me a large clean white handkerchief on which to blow my nose. He was looking at me solemnly.

'Maybe you're still suffering from shock,' he said at last.

I sniffed and blew once more.

'Shock?' I repeated.

'From yesterday – the car accident,' he explained.

'Oh, that! It didn't bother me.'

But I wondered if Allan could be right. I fancied myself as a fairly controlled person one way and another. I certainly did not give way to wild impulses to be rude to total strangers and then weep my remorse out on their shoulders. Perhaps I *was* suffering from shock. I repeated my thoughts aloud. He seemed to agree with me.

'The same might be said for me,' he said dryly as we started walking again. 'I'm not in the habit of kissing strange girls either!'

I smiled. Suddenly I liked him very much indeed; not in a romantic way, just *liked* him. He could be a good friend, I thought. It was a pity he was an American.

'When do you go back to the States?' I asked. 'Soon?'

'Oh no, you won't get rid of me as quickly as that,' he laughed. 'I'm over here for six months. I lecture on Forestry and I've got leave from my university to prepare a thesis for a further degree I aim to take. I hope to spend all of it in England. I like the country and the people and I've nothing to hurry home for.'

'No wife? No fiancée?'

He shook his head, stopping for a moment to throw a stick for the eager Bramble to retrieve.

'No wife. There was a fiancée but we called it quits a year ago. And you?'

Suddenly I was telling him about Peter – not just the facts but my hurt feelings and Peter's erratic correspondence, the lot.

'I think it's just a matter of time before Peter and I will be calling it quits too,' I finished. 'Perhaps we were engaged too long. I don't know and I'm not sure that I care.'

'But deep down you do,' Allan said shrewdly. 'Maybe he'll find he misses you and will come home. Or send for you. Even if he has to keep his bachelor status, you could still go out there. Didn't you think of doing that?'

'I thought of it all right,' I said bitterly. 'But the fare costs money and Peter didn't think we should waste our savings that way. And don't tell me I'm crazy to love a man like that – I know it. I just can't help it. I've loved him for years.'

I suppose I'm no more selfish than the average – usually – but that afternoon I talked non stop about Peter; what he meant to me, where and how we had met, things we had done and planned to do. I must have bored Allan stiff but he never gave a sign of it, only nodding now and again to show he was listening. Getting it all off my chest was wonderful therapy for me and for the time brought Peter very near again in thought at least.

Later, when Allan had driven off in his hired Mini back to the small hotel in Goodwood where he was living, I thought over the afternoon again and realised what a crashing bore I must have been. It would not have surprised me in the very least if I'd seen the last of him. I didn't particularly care that I'd queered my pitch with him but in a vague kind of way I was sorry.

The following morning, however, he telephoned to invite me to go walking with him in West Dean Park. I was pleased and a little flattered, until I reminded myself that he was probably pretty lonely, a stranger in a strange country where no doubt even my company was better than none. I refused the invitation, though, because as I told him, I had a lot of typing to catch up on.

'Then how about dinner tonight?' he persisted. 'They don't do anything very special here but we could go out somewhere.'

I hesitated, not sure if I wanted to spend a whole evening with him. I'd grown used to my quiet evenings alone with Lady Barclay, reading my book and occasionally exchanging the odd remark while she worked on her tapestry until bedtime. Did I want to come out of my rut? I'd thought so that day I'd driven down to Brighton and had so much fun with Simon. Somehow time spent with Simon meant fun. With Allan I was forced to think and feel and my barriers of reserve were broken down.

The decision was taken out of my hands by Lady Barclay who was listening to the one sided conversation.

'Invite that young man to supper with us.

I have a great deal I want to ask him.'

I had no alternative but to pass on the invitation which Allan jumped at. He rang off, sounding pleased with life.

'I don't know if we should have him here,' I remarked tersely. 'After all, we don't know anything about him, Lady Barclay, and there's no one in the house but ourselves and that old couple downstairs.'

To my chagrin, Lady Barclay laughed.

'My dear child, I've lived long enough to be a reasonably good judge of my fellow human beings. That young man is as honest as they come. I'd trust him in exactly the same way as I trust you.'

The hidden dig was justified. When Lady Barclay met me, she had not asked for references, stranger though I was, but had taken me equally on trust.

'You don't like him very much, do you?' she said thoughtfully. 'I wonder why.'

It was not a question but I did give an answer.

'I think he is too good to be true,' I said flatly. 'He is just a bit *too* nice. I can't explain exactly.'

Again Lady Barclay laughed.

'No facts to back your opinion, Jenny? Then we might as well assume he is as nice as we've found him to be until he proves otherwise.'

That ended the conversation. I retired to my room – a beautiful oblong bedroom in the north wing of the house filled with the mellowness of lovely faded old brocade and furniture bright with the polish of centuries.

I sat down on the bed and picked up the framed photograph of Peter I kept on the table beneath the reading lamp. His face stared back at me, unsmiling, a face I knew so very well and had loved for so long. A dear, familiar, loving face, I thought. But was it? Was that long, beautifully shaped mouth really just that or was there a hint of meanness, of cruelty about the lips? Were those unsmiling eyes hiding a true generosity of spirit or a quiet selfishness? Was that line of cheekbone strong with determination or merely with ambition? Did I really know him at all?

Suddenly I felt utterly miserable and alone. In a few short weeks Peter had turned into a stranger. If he were to walk into the room now would I want to throw myself into his arms with hysterical delight or would I much prefer to vent some of my hurt and angry humiliation on him, the cause of it? I didn't know. I wasn't sure. I wasn't even sure if I still loved him. I thought I must or else I wouldn't care so terribly about him forsaking me. And that's how I felt – completely forsaken. Was I nursing a broken heart or shattered pride?

I wished very much that Allan Howe was not coming to supper, and even toyed with the idea of excusing myself on some pretext. I resented his intrusion into our comfortable little evenings in which Lady Barclay and I could talk or not, just as we liked. Now we would both have to make polite conversation to the guest. Even as the thought crossed my mind I knew it wasn't true. Lady Barclay had not had to 'make conversation' at lunchtime yesterday and nor had I. Allan was easy to talk to.

And there, I pointed out to myself, lay the root cause of my objection. I had bared my soul to Allan, thinking he would stay a stranger and now I had to face him again with the wound still gaping. I hated the idea that I had given him the chance to pity me as a stupid girl whose fiancé had rejected her and who hadn't the guts to call the engagement off. He would know me as no one else down here at the Manor knew me, as weak and spineless, wanting a man who didn't want me. I would have given anything to withdraw those confidences, spilled out so stupidly and thoughtlessly yesterday afternoon in the woods. Until then I had kept my feelings well under control – so well under control, in fact, that I hadn't allowed myself to be conscious of my thoughts, let alone given voice to them. And by being the way he was, he, Allan, had tricked me into facing the truth and admitting it. Peter just did not love me. Now I knew it as well as Allan.

Impulsively, I reacted. I sat down at my desk and wrote to Peter, telling him I no longer wanted to marry him; that our engagement was off and that with no hard feelings I was saying goodbye and wished him well. I addressed the envelope and sealed it quickly before I could change my mind.

In the same mood I went down to join Lady Barclay and Allan who had already arrived, and accepted the glass of sherry she offered me. I raised the glass and with considerable dramatic affect, said brightly:

'I'd like to propose a toast. To my regained freedom. I have just broken my engagement.'

Lady Barclay looked astonished. She knew about Peter, of course, for every evening and quite without shame, I had used her as a pair of ears in which to pour endless stories of Peter's and my life together. Naturally she thought he was wonderful since it was in that light I always presented him. She believed, too, that he was as madly in love with me as I was with him, because that is what I wanted her to believe. No wonder she looked shattered.

'My dear!' she broke a long silence. 'You don't really mean that, do you?'

'Oh, yes, I do!' My bright little laugh wasn't too bad. 'You know how these things are – here today and gone tomorrow!'

I was horrified to realise how near to tears I was. My remark sounded fatuous even to me and I gulped down my sherry quickly. Of course it had to be Allan Howe to the rescue. He was saying to Lady Barclay:

'I think Jennifer is sensible not to tie herself down while she is still so young. Don't you think, Lady Barclay, that long engagements are a mistake? They sure put an awful strain on any relationship. I believe people should remain free until they really do feel ready to settle down to marriage. That's why I broke off my own engagement. I just wasn't ready for it and nor was Sue. She married somebody else a month ago which proves we were both right.'

Cunningly he swung the conversation away from Peter and me to himself, diverting Lady Barclay with the saga of his past romance. He was telling her in detail all about Sue and their affair which had begun and ended at university.

I didn't listen very hard. I was too busy trying to get myself under control. The enormity of the step I had taken was only just getting through to me. I had ended my engagement to Peter! True, I could rush upstairs and burn that letter – but I knew I wouldn't. By telling the two people in the room I had burned my boats, so to speak. I wouldn't go back on it and wasn't even sure if I wanted to. As Allan said, I was free now. And if Peter did really love me the way I wanted him to, he could prove it by putting up a fight – perhaps even come home and argue with me face to face.

The dinner gong sounded and still partly dazed, I followed Lady Barclay into the dining-room. Yesterday in the woods, Allan had said that my emotion was just shock reaction to the accident. Perhaps he was right for I couldn't think of any other reason for my utterly unprecedented and unwarranted loss of emotional control. Since the day Peter left, I had behaved absolutely normally and rationally, as if nothing disastrous had occurred. There had to be some reason for reacting like this now, weeks later.

I looked across the table, glowing softly in candlelight and found Allan's eyes on me. The look of anxiety gave way to a questioning smile. Suddenly I liked him again. He was thoughtful and kind. Slowly and almost reluctantly I found myself returning his smile.

At that moment the telephone rang. Lady Barclay and I looked at each other in surprise. It was seldom anyone rang up when we were alone at the Manor. I went off to answer it. It was Simon – for me.

'Hello, sweetie!' His half bantering tone brought back a vivid picture of him. I could almost see him standing by me, grinning down with that teasing smile in his eyes. 'Didn't get a chance to say goodbye to you in the rush back to town on Monday. How's things? No ill effects from our little car episode, I trust?'

'No, I'm fine, thanks, and incidentally, your "victim" is dining here. He doesn't appear to bear you any malice.'

There was a brief pause before Simon spoke again. When he did there was a slight edge to his voice.

'The American fellow? He's there – with you?'

There was no mistaking the jealous undertone. I felt a little thrill of pleasure. It was nice to feel a man being possessive.

'Well, actually Lady Barclay invited him. They've become great buddies.'

Simon still sounded peeved as he said:

'Well, so long as it's only the Old Trout who's got an eye on him, I don't care. I'm relying on you, Jennifer, to remain strictly faithful to me.'

I knew he was teasing, of course, but I began to enjoy myself. It was a long time since I'd had the fun of playing games with words.

'Well, I can't promise to be faithful to anyone,' I replied, 'especially when it's not very likely they are being faithful to me. Which of those beautiful girls did you drive back to London?'

'If you must know, none of them. I drove alone, Jennifer. Alone and thinking of you. A tantalising memory.'

'Why tantalising?' I laughed.

'Because, damn it, that's exactly what you are – one minute all promise and the next the cold shoulder.'

'That's nonsense!' I told him. 'I was never anything but friendly until you propositioned me and then what did you expect? That I'd fall into your open arms. We'd only known each other one day, Simon.'

'So what? A day is long enough to know if you're in love. I'm crazy about you. You must know that. I'm coming down next weekend – without the gang. I want you all to myself.'

The banter had left his voice but I didn't take him seriously. After all, people don't 'fall in love' at first sight – certainly not people like Simon. I doubted very much if he knew what the word meant. All the same, I was flattered to think he was attracted to me. In a way I was attracted to him too. I wasn't sure if I actually *liked* him but he did interest and intrigue me. There was something a little dangerous about him that I found irresistible. It was a long time since I'd played with fire and I was revelling in it. Now I had broken my engagement I was free to flirt with anyone I chose. I'd show Peter just how little he mattered!

'I'll look forward to seeing you!' I said honestly. 'But, Simon, no more ton-ups. I'd rather live!'

'Well, get the Old Trout organised so

you're free to be with me when I get down. I'll try for Friday night after work. Okay?'

I didn't like him calling my dear old Lady Barclay 'the Old Trout'. I was genuinely fond of her and his lack of respect jarred. I was about to tell him so when I remembered that we had only just begun dinner and I had been away a long time. I said goodbye hastily and scuttled back to the dining-room.

'The call was for me. I'm sorry to have been so long,' I said. I don't know why I didn't tell them it was Simon on the other end of the 'phone but I didn't. Lady Barclay was far too well mannered to question me; and it was none of Allan's business.

For the rest of the evening I was tittering with excitement, monopolising the conversation and talking and laughing far too much. Once or twice I caught Allan eyeing me with a puzzled expression as if surprised to see this side of the quiet little Jenny of yesterday. At least, I told myself with satisfaction, he can't be seeing me as a broken-hearted tearful girl that Peter didn't want! I had the feeling that Allan did not approve of this new me. Not that I cared what he thought. Why should I? I just wished that I had not made such an idiot of myself yesterday. I certainly didn't want to remember that kiss and I hoped he'd forgotten it – along with my tears and my maudlin confessions. After all, I had had no option of refusing it. He'd kissed me before I'd realised what was happening. Why? I couldn't think of any reason except the infuriating one that he felt sorry for me.

Allan did not stay late. He left soon after coffee and obeying Lady Barclay's instructions, I saw him to the door. We were alone in the great hall and I shivered, feeling suddenly cold and depressed. The evening had gone flat.

'I hope you weren't too bored!' I said.

Again, Allan gave me one of those puzzled looks. He didn't seem to like my flippancy.

'Don't be sad, Jenny!' he said.

His words enraged me. Did he imagine I wanted his pity? And I wasn't sad. He had no right at all to make such personal remarks.

'I'm not,' I told him. 'I'm on top of the world and rightly. Simon is coming down next weekend – it was he who telephoned. I'm looking forward to it.'

An odd look went over Allan's face. I did not know him well enough to interpret it but I did wonder, just for a moment, if somehow or other I had upset him. Then he smiled and said:

'That'll be nice for you. He seemed a lively kind of guy. By the way, Jenny, that cottage of yours – Lady Barclay says you want to let it. She suggests I take it for the six months I'm over here – that is, if you approve of me as a tenant?'

My depression plunged even deeper. Lodge Cottage – our home, Peter's and mine. I had made no effort to press the agents to find tenants. In my heart I didn't want anyone else to live there. It held so many of my hopes and plans – our plans. We'd saved so long and gone without so much to buy it. I hadn't been able to bring myself to go near it while I was at the Manor. When I took Bramble for walks or left the house for any reason, I always made a point of going down the back drive.

I suppose Allan had seen the To Let sign in the little garden as he drove in through the main gate. He must have questioned Lady Barclay about it. There was no valid reason why he shouldn't rent it, but I knew I didn't want him there – nor anyone else. At the back of my mind I think I must have been hoping that Peter would suddenly come back to England and that *we* would live there as we'd always planned. Economically, of course, it should have been let the moment Peter left the country and we'd known we weren't going to need it for at least two years.

'I can't give you an answer,' I told Allan. 'It's in the hands of the agents and for all I know they may have let it already. And now that we aren't going to get married after all, Peter may want to sell the place.'

Allan voiced his disappointment.

'It's a real picture postcard cottage,' he said. 'I fell in love with it the first time I saw it. I'm sorry. If the chance does come up, will you let me know? I'd take care of the place. As a matter of fact, I'm quite a keen gardener. I'd keep it in order.'

'Yes, well...' I broke off, feeling desolate and miserable. Oh, Peter! I cried inside me. The letter was still not posted. I could tear it up ... let things alone. Had I really the strength or the will to challenge his love in this way? For that was what I was doing – challenging him to prove he loved me better than anything else.

I suddenly realised I had been standing there lost in thought and gawping like some stupid half-wit. I managed a smile and held out my hand to bid Allan goodnight.

He took it but did not shake it. He just

held it. Mine was cold and shaking. His felt very warm and firm. I pulled mine away.

'Goodnight!' I said abruptly, and opened the front door.

He did not turn his head, but disappeared into the darkness, his Mini puttering into the night, the twin headlights casting sharp beams of light on the white gravel as it wound its way down the tree-lined drive.

I turned away, shivering violently, and was glad to get back to the comfortable familiarity of the sitting-room. The rest of the evening passed as usual, with Lady Barclay stitching away at her tapestry and I with my nose in a book, turning the pages when I thought of it.

4

Simon did not, after all, come down that next weekend. He telephoned to say that some really urgent business had cropped up and he just could not get away. He sounded as genuinely disappointed as I was. I asked Lady Barclay what kind of a job Simon had.

'I couldn't tell you, my dear,' she said. 'He

did work for a while in some shipping firm. My brother got him the job when he came back from America but Simon did not like it. There was talk of him going into politics but of course that came to nothing. He hadn't the right background.'

I was curious.

'Surely with his stepfather behind him…?' I began but Lady Barclay broke in.

'I'm afraid that wouldn't have helped. You see, Jenny, there was the unfortunate episode at his public-school – it was never actually a scandal – my brother saw to that – but a politician can't afford even a hint of scandal in his past. I suppose you wouldn't know about it.'

I shook my head.

'Well, there is no harm in your knowing – it might be a good thing that you should. Simon was in his teens at the time. He and another boy were involved in a shooting accident. The other boy was killed.'

'But how terrible!' I said. 'And it was Simon's fault?'

The old lady nodded.

'There was an inquest, of course. Unfortunately, Simon was known to have a grudge against the other boy – older than himself – who had reported Simon for breaking some rule and got him into trouble with the head master. The boy's parents knew about it and kept insisting that Simon had intended their son's death. Simon's story was that the older boy had challenged him to a shooting match and had walked into the line of fire. It couldn't be proved or disproved.'

'But of course it must have been an accident!' I said. 'How could anyone think anything else? A schoolboy doesn't murder another boy because he got him into trouble with his head master. It's absurd!'

'That was the line Simon's lawyer took. Simon was only fifteen at the time. I didn't attend the court, of course, but my brother told me afterwards that Simon made a very good impression when he gave evidence on his own behalf. He admitted quite openly that there had been ill feeling between himself and the other boy and he had felt justifiably upset when this boy sneaked on him to the Head. But since all he had done was to break the rule that boys should not be off the premises after nine at night, all the punishment given him was a curtailing of his free time and he pointed out it was not likely he would want to commit murder for something as unimportant as that. Nor was it likely the boy would have arranged to be alone with him on a shooting range if he felt Simon bore any grudge against him.'

'So he was exonerated?'

Lady Barclay nodded.

'He had to leave the school, of course, and neither my brother nor Julia felt like risking a possible refusal to take him by another school. They sent him to America instead.'

'But if he was proved innocent, why did he have to leave?' I asked.

'My brother did try to persuade the head master to keep him on, but he said that after all the talk there had been it would be neither in Simon's best interest nor the school's if he agreed. Since Simon's school record was not of the best my brother did not feel justified in pulling strings with the governors. Julia wanted him to leave, anyway, so that was that.'

It seemed very unfair to me. If anyone was to blame it was the school for allowing boys of that age to fool around with guns without a master there to keep an eye on them. It must have had a terrible effect on Simon – having to live with the knowledge he had killed another boy, even if it was an accident.

I found myself wondering about Lord Barclay's feelings for his stepson. There was no doubt Julia doted on Simon but Lord Barclay's attitude towards him didn't sound too good. No wonder Simon was a bit wild, I thought as I trailed up to bed. I must ask him next time I saw him what kind of job he was doing.

I lay in bed making comparisons between Simon and Allan. There could be only a year or two's difference in their ages and yet I thought of Simon as a boy and of Allan as a man. It didn't make sense for of the two, Simon was by far the more sophisticated. It was that quiet steadiness in Allan that made one think he was older than he really was. Simon was a far more exciting personality. I couldn't quite bring myself to use the description 'dull' for Allan because he was too intelligent ever to be dull. I couldn't call him unprovocative either, for he certainly succeeded in provoking me. But where Simon made me laugh, Allan made me think and I didn't want to think.

I carefully avoided looking at the letter to Peter lying on my beside table. I made myself two promises – one, that I would post that letter first thing in the morning and two, that I wasn't going to see Allan Howe again if I could prevent it. In a funny way, he reminded me of Peter, not to look at, but in type. I finally drifted into sleep on the bitter reminder to myself: 'Once bitten, twice shy!'

The Crimson Tapestry was making good progress. Left to ourselves, Lady Barclay and I were slowly piling up completed chapters of the book. We had no interruptions to divert us. Allan telephoned once inviting me to lunch but I made the excuse that I was busy. Simon telephoned twice – not for any purpose I could fathom except to have a verbal flirtation with me, which was harmless and fun. I was looking forward to his arrival at the weekend and hoped that this time pressure of work would not stop him coming.

We were now engrossed in a chapter of the Barclay history dealing with the Battle of Trafalgar. Lady Barclay asked me to go into Chichester to do some research for her. I enjoyed these occasional sessions of poring over great worn volumes in the reference section of the Public Library. It was a kind of treasure hunt in which I nosed out the details she wanted. Usually I never saw a soul I knew but on this occasion I had to come face to face with Allan. He said he was doing some research, too, and seemed almost as familiar with the library facilities as I was.

Since it was nearly twelve-thirty when we recognised each other, I could hardly say I had already lunched, and obviously at this hour, did not intend returning to the Manor for the meal. I had no reasonable excuse for refusing Allan's invitation to lunch with him and an unreasonable one would not do. For one thing, he looked so anxious when he was asking me, as if expecting a refusal, and so relieved when I said I would.

We went to an old pub Allan knew where we washed down a wonderful game pie with beer served in pewter mugs. He was plainly delighted with the place and pleased when I said I liked it too. I could see why he liked it. Americans love old English pubs and this one was less spoilt and more traditional than most.

He didn't, as I had half feared, refer to Peter but talked smoothly and easily about a charcoal burner he'd met in West Dean Park.

'He showed me exactly how he produced the stuff.' Allan sounded as excited as a schoolboy with a new stamp for his collection. 'He has four great iron pots – one must have been at least nine feet in diameter. It made me think of a huge witch's cauldron. He cooks the wood in these pots for three days. It used to be done in sort of pyramids of timber but the pots are better because it's easier to control the draught; though even then it's quite an art and a job to prevent too much oxygen getting in.'

I was beginning to get interested.

'What happens if there is too much air?' I asked.

'Well, the wood would just burn away instead of charring,' Allan said. 'This chap, Leonard Turner, lives in a caravan on the site so he can keep an eye on it all the time. I asked him if he didn't feel lonely all by himself in the woods but he says he's quite at home there.'

'And the finished product?' I asked. 'What happens to that?'

Allan ordered coffee and lit a cigarette before he answered. I was getting used to the smell of American tobacco and though he didn't smoke often, it seemed very much a part of him now.

'The charcoal is bagged and collected for delivery by a chemical firm called I.C.I. I've taken some wonderful photographs, Jennifer. They're being developed right now and I sure do hope they'll come out well. You've never seen such lovely trees – old as the hills, some of them. Better even than your Manor park trees where we walked the other afternoon.'

I didn't want to be reminded of that day. The thought of my stupid tears and Allan's kiss was still an embarrassment to me. I finished my coffee quickly and said I must get back to work.

The hour of easy talk and companionship was spoiled and as Allan walked back to the library with me, I decided once again to put an end to this friendship. I had a shrewd idea he would ask me to lunch again and rehearsed an answer. When his invitation came I was ready:

'I'm afraid I just can't commit myself to any date, Allan. I'm supposed to be on call whenever Lady Barclay wants me. I don't have regular hours on and off work.'

I was sure he knew I was making excuses. After all he knew just how sweet and kind my old lady was. It was extremely unlikely she would refuse me time off to lunch with Allan whom she liked. But he took the hint. He just said:

'Well, maybe we'll run into each other again soon. I hope so. Goodbye, Jenny.'

I felt vaguely upset. I didn't like hurting anyone and the expression on Allan's face was distinctly that of someone who had recognised and accepted a rebuff. He was obviously lonely and it was not very nice of me. But I couldn't help it. I just did not want to get involved.

My friendship with Simon, however, took great leaps forward over the weekend. He arrived late on Friday when I had almost given up hope of him coming, and Lady Barclay had already gone to bed. He was in great form. He came into my room where I was passing the time in correcting the day's typing, lifted me out of my chair as if I was a child, and swung me round in a circle, his green eyes full of laughter.

'How's my favourite girl friend?' he asked, and without waiting for a reply, kissed me on both cheeks like a Frenchman and held me prisoner at arm's length while he studied my face.

'Prettier than ever. You have a most beautiful skin, Jennifer. Peaches and cream, the poets would say. Camay, T.V. would claim. Lovely, either way.'

I laughed with him. It was so easy to be amused by Simon.

He looked very smart in a tailored suit and

silk shirt. The perfectly cut trousers made his long legs look even longer. He might well have stepped out of one of the Barclay portraits – but of course he was not a Barclay.

We went downstairs where he first rifled the sideboard for whisky and then raided the fridge in the kitchen for what he wanted.

'That's probably tomorrow's lunch!' I protested as he sat on the edge of the table gnawing hungrily on the cold carcase of a pheasant.

'Then they'll have to find something else, won't they?' Simon shrugged. 'That's one thing I've learned in my short life, Jennifer, love – never ask – just take. People don't hang around waiting to give you things. You've got to grab what you want and hang on to it.'

The bitterness in his voice disturbed me. He noticed my slight frown and laughed.

'My dear little innocent, don't look so reproachful. Just consider a little while and you'll see that I'm right. The soft ones go under – people use and abuse them. You've got to fit into one category or the other – the user or the used.'

My thoughts were never very far away from Peter and now they flew to the years I'd devoted to him. Perhaps Simon was right. I had given everything to Peter – as much love as I was capable of giving any man. And where had it got me? Peter simply did not value me at all. If I had been a little harder … less giving … more demanding…

'So now, my adored one, since you are one of Nature's givers and I am one of Nature's takers, how about giving me the kiss I'm going to take anyway?'

He was teasing again but I knew by the tiny shiver that went through me that he meant to have what he wanted. I backed away from him.

'But you've just told me it doesn't pay to be a giver!' I told him, using the same bantering tone he had used to hide my confusion. 'And I've decided you are absolutely right. So I'll say goodnight and look forward to seeing you in the morning.'

I didn't get away with it. Simon was off the table and had covered the few feet between us before I reached the kitchen door. His arms went round me and his mouth came down on mine smothering my feeble half-hearted protest.

My emotions were completely at sea. There was an element in Simon's kisses that frightened me. At the same time I felt myself weakening, responding and finally returning them with equal passion. In a matter of minutes we were both breathless and I was really having to fight to push Simon away before we became caught up in something much deeper than I wanted.

'Don't Simon, don't!' I gasped. 'I don't want it ... I don't want to...'

He was staring at me with green eyes narrowed and blazing. I thought that at any moment the two hands gripping my arms so fiercely, would drag me back against him and that I would be lost, helpless. We stared at one another for what seemed eternity. Then suddenly he smiled and let me go.

'Perhaps you're right!' he said. 'Perhaps it's a hell of a lot more fun your way. But you're going to end up mine, Jennifer – *mine!*'

I stood silent and helpless. Seeing Simon like this, feeling the force of his passion and more frightening, the force of my own, I did not find it hard to believe him. I had never experienced such a tide of pure physical desire. I was more physically attracted to Simon then I'd been to any man ever – even to Peter. And Simon was three parts a stranger.

Simon was once more sitting on the edge of the table. He was watching my face.

'I haven't been able to get you out of my

mind,' he said, more to himself than to me. 'For two damned long weeks I've kept seeing you in my mind. I don't know what it is about you. You're different from the others. I've never wanted any girl the way I want you. Perhaps it's that innocent look and yet I'll swear you're as full of passion as I am. You're not really beautiful, you know. I've seen a dozen girls prettier. But you've got something ... something that's driving me to distraction. Better get off to your bed quickly – before I take you to mine.'

'Don't!' I whispered, the plea coming from me before I could think about it. 'Don't spoil things, Simon.'

His eyebrows shot up.

'Spoil things?'

I nodded.

'The way you're talking. You're reducing everything to – to...'

'Oh, I see!' Simon broke in. 'You're a romantic. You want the icing on the cake! Well, so be it. You can have it any way you want, Jennifer. Love and roses. I'll court you, if that's what you want. Send you flowers, write you little letters. I can play that game if I have to.'

'Simon, I don't want to play any game. I just want...' I searched for the right words to express my feelings. 'I just want us to be friends!'

'Oh, Jennifer!' His voice sounded almost reproachful. 'Time you woke up, sweetie. What's between us isn't *friendship* ... it's the kind of thing that happens between a man and a woman and nothing in the whole wide world will stop it. You can put up a fight, if you want, but it won't last. It can't.'

He frightened me – making the future seem fated, out of control. Besides, in my heart I didn't agree with him. Sex couldn't be divorced from love – at least, I didn't want it to be. I certainly did not go along with the modern view that sex for its own sake was important. I wanted to love, or at least I wanted more than passion in any relationship in which I became involved. Why couldn't we be friends?

Unknowingly I must have spoken the last thought aloud for Simon said:

'Because nature didn't intend it, luv. The battle of the sexes, you know.'

I was suddenly dispirited. My moment of weakness had passed and I felt stronger, better able to deal with the situation.

'I'm going to bed, Simon,' I said quietly. 'I'm sorry if I can't see things your way and I don't agree that the future is out of our control. I intend to control my life and what I do with it. So at least we can begin honestly. I know what you want of me and you know that this is not what I want of you. Okay?'

To my chagrin, Simon smiled.

'You've just agreed with me, sweetie – the battle of the sexes. I'm accepting your terms – we fight it out. But I shall win, Jennifer. I shall win. It's my policy in life always to get what I want.'

Just to show him that he wasn't winning this round anyway, I turned and left him without even bothering to say goodnight.

5

I suppose my life had been lived fairly much in a backwater since Peter had left England and me behind him. Now suddenly, events were carrying me along with such rapidity that I was jolted out of my comfortable little hiding place.

First and foremost, by the Saturday morning post, came a letter from Peter. The shock I might have felt had it come a week earlier was only slightly tempered by the fact that I had come to the same conclusion as Peter – that our engagement was better ended. Nevertheless, it *was* a shock, for at the back of my mind, I wanted to leave a door open through which Peter could if he wished, re-enter my life. Now I was forced to face the fact that this was both improbable and unlikely.

It was a dismal apologetic letter – one I imagine he had found hard to write. It was full of platitudes – *'I hope you will find it in your heart to understand and forgive'* – that kind of thing. But the cold facts were there – Peter had met another girl and wanted to be free to pursue this new interest without feelings of disloyalty to me. He didn't say much about her – perhaps from tact, but it was obvious he was already crazy about her the way he had not felt about me in years.

'Don't you agree, Jenny,' he wrote, *'that of late we were drifting into marriage as a matter of course rather than because either of us felt it was the most important thing in the world to us...'*

That made me bitter. Peter might not have felt it the most important thing in the world but how could he have doubted my feelings? Yet there was a tiny seed of truth – we had drifted. But that had been Peter's fault rather than mine!

My emotions were turbulent to say the least. I was hurt, angry, disillusioned, bitter and at the same time, honest enough to accept that I had written on very similar lines to Peter and, maybe, not for so very different a reason – I had met Simon who attracted me far more than Peter had ever done. Good or bad, I found Simon incredibly attractive. How could I profess to love Peter with my whole heart whilst I could react to another man in such a way?

My self questioning continued, as I sought the truth. I did not want to feel bitter towards Peter and yet it was his behaviour towards me that had brought about this change in our relationship – not mine towards him. I was the faithful type; I'd have married him and lived happily ever after in the Lodge cottage if ... but what was the use of 'ifs'? I could see now that Peter had welcomed that posting overseas as a subconscious way out of an engagement that had gone on too long. How blind I had been! How stupidly trusting!

I went down to breakfast in a none-too-good frame of mind. Hurt, I wanted to hurt someone in return and I ignored Simon's welcoming smile and pulled my arm away childishly as he laid a hand on my wrist. He sat down opposite me and pushed the large packet of cornflakes towards me.

'Obviously not at your best at breakfast time!' he remarked laconically. 'I've made a mental note!'

'Don't be silly!' I said crossly, pouring far too much milk on my cereal. I was relieved to see Lady Barclay come into the dining-room. She nodded good morning to Simon and immediately engaged me in conversation. Surprisingly, she wanted me to work all morning. I had thought I was up to date with the typing. However, she found some notes in longhand she wished me to type and naturally I was at her disposal.

Simon was annoyed. I could not help but see the swift look of irritation he sent in Lady Barclay's direction. He opened his mouth as if he intended to speak but closed it again, obviously having decided not to antagonise the old lady. He finished his breakfast and stood up.

'I'll see you at lunch, Jennifer!' he said. 'Perhaps this afternoon you'll be off duty. I thought we might drive into Goodwood whilst I still have my licence.'

Lady Barclay did not look up from her

plate although I knew she heard him. She waited till he had left before she turned to me and said:

'Of course, I can't prevent you doing what you wish with your free time, my dear, but for your own sake I would be much happier if you did not let Simon monopolise you.'

'He's not such a bad driver!' I replied, deliberately misunderstanding her. 'But if it will make you easier in your mind, I'll do the driving.'

She looked so hurt and bewildered that I almost weakened. I wanted to say I was sorry and ask her to try to understand that Simon wasn't really the black sheep she believed him to be; that I was quite capable of managing him; and moreover, that after the knock I had had from Peter this morning, I didn't want to be by myself.

Pride, coupled with the fact that I was not sure enough of the reason for my own behaviour, made me reluctant to confide in her. Perhaps one of the reasons for my reticence was that I knew very well that she disliked Simon and had no wish to hear her reiterate her feelings towards him. In any event, I stayed silent and left the room as quickly as I could before my poor Lady B. could begin to undermine my resolve to enjoy myself this afternoon no matter what.

I was not the only one in a determined mood. Simon had clearly made up his mind that he would succeed in convincing me of the seriousness of his feelings for me.

He drove me towards Goodwood at a steady forty miles an hour, ('to please you, sweetie,' he had said grinning, 'and not to placate the Old Trout'). After that he was silent for some miles and when at last he did speak, it was to say:

'I know you think I'm just a good-time Charlie, Jennifer. Maybe that's not so far off the truth up to now. But the way I feel about you – it's different to the way I've ever felt about any girl, and that's the truth, believe it or not.'

There was a different note in his voice – a more genuine sincerity in it that was convincing. I didn't want to get serious so I tried flippancy.

'Bet you say that to all the girls!'

He ignored my remark.

'I've played around, Jennifer – as much or more than most men of my age. I'm not denying I've anything like a clean slate. But then I've never before felt it was worth while sticking to the old accepted clichés – faithfulness, one boy one girl, that kind of thing.

Damn it all, what I'm trying to say is that I've fallen in love with you. I suppose you'll laugh now.'

But I didn't want to laugh. I felt instinctively that Simon believed what he was saying even if I did not yet believe that he really was 'in love'. We'd known each other an absurdly short time and he knew next to nothing about me – the real deep-down-inside me. I thought he was confusing love with attraction and I told him so.

'You're a romantic!' he argued. 'There's no such thing as love without physical attraction. Of course I'm attracted to you. Why the hell do you think I've packed in all my other girl friends and stayed home nights if it's not because I'm incapable of thinking about anyone *but* you. You don't have any idea, obviously, what you've done to me. I can't look at you without wanting you. Is that so terrible?'

'No, not terrible,' I said slowly, trying to keep a grip on my emotions. I was, after all, only human and Simon's words were balm to the wound Peter had inflicted. At least one man thought me desirable above all other women even if Peter did not!

But at the same time, I was cautious enough to be aware of the fact that I was very vulnerable. This was just the psychological moment for me to rebound. I told Simon so.

'That's why I'd rather you didn't take me seriously – or be serious about me,' I pleaded. 'Can't we just be friends, Simon? Have fun together without … without…'

'Without sex rearing its ugly head? I doubt it. I don't believe in platonic relationships, and certainly not with you. But I'll play it any way you want, Jennifer. No jumping into bed if that's what you're afraid of. But don't ask me not to kiss you, touch you, make love to you. Am I really that unattractive to you?'

'No, of course not, and you know it!' I said. It seemed ridiculous to pretend otherwise. Whatever kind of relationship emerged, I didn't want any more beating about the bush – letting things drift, discussing a future and forgetting to discuss the all-important present. That is what had happened between Peter and me. We'd been so busy planning where to live, how to save money to buy a house, which house, what carpet, when we'd marry, that we'd forgotten to ask each other if we still wanted to get married. I'd be wiser this time. Not that I had even started to think of Simon in terms of marriage. I just wanted to understand what was developing and know what I had to contend with. There would be no more shocks for me.

'What did you think of my mother, Jennifer?'

The unexpectedness of Simon's question pulled me swiftly out of my thoughts.

'I didn't really see much of her the one time she was at the Manor,' I said truthfully. 'I thought she was very attractive.'

'She thinks you are!' Simon said. She agrees with me absolutely about you. You know, Jennifer, it surprised me a little that she should feel so warmly towards you. I always thought she had it at the back of her mind to marry me off to some rich American girl – or a title or something!' He laughed a shade bitterly. 'She never really got over the fact that my fond stepfather won't acknowledge me.'

'But, Simon, he does. I'm sure he does. Old Lady Barclay was telling me that…'

'Oh, yes, I get lip service. He hasn't publicly disowned me, if that's what you mean. But there was talk years ago of his making me his heir. I couldn't inherit the house, of course, or the title, but he told Mama he'd leave everything else to me that wasn't a family heirloom or entailed. To tell you the truth, Jennifer, I think Mother married him partly in order to secure my future. He's a hell of a lot older than she is and – well, you could hardly call the old boy attractive, to put it mildly.'

'She didn't love him, then?'

The hint of reproach must have shown itself in my voice for Simon said flatly:

'You are an innocent little idealist, aren't you? No, I don't think she loved him but she was prepared to be a good wife to him. Until he rejected me she was, too. It's his own fault they live more or less separate private lives now. After all, it was only natural I should come first.'

I said nothing, remembering, as I'm sure Simon was, the unfortunate story of his public school episode. I was beginning to feel more sympathetic towards Simon and less than ever in agreement with old Lady Barclay's view that Simon had been a black sheep. To withdraw affection, even that of a stepfather, from an adolescent boy just at the one time when he was having to face up to serious trouble, was not conducive to making a child stable or 'good'. And to reject him even after his innocence had been established was like a betrayal – a way of saying: 'Others might think you're innocent but I believe you guilty.'

'When Mother discovered he'd cut me out of the proverbial Will, she turned against him,' Simon was saying. 'She's put money aside for me in her own Will and there's nothing the old boy can do about it. He gives her an allowance and what she does with it is her affair. But it's not much and I know Mother was and still is bitter about it. That's why I was hesitant in telling her how I felt about you. The wonderful thing is that she more than understands – and approves, Jennifer. She really likes you.'

Just for a moment, I felt uneasy. After all, how could Julia judge me on so short an acquaintance? I couldn't pass judgement on her. Why should Simon's mother want to encourage him to take any kind of interest in me, of all insignificant people?

Yet almost at once, I felt I did understand. One had only to recall the hard drinking, fast living, brittle quality of the young women in Simon's 'crowd' who'd turned up for the weekend to know the kind of girl Simon usually dated. It was natural for a mother to want above all for the girl her son eventually married to be capable of loving him, maybe even of steering him towards a quieter, more worth while life; to counter balance the 'wild' streak in him. A nice, steady, hard-working, dependable, sensible girl! That was no doubt the way she saw me. And a day or two ago, the description wouldn't have been so far from the truth. But now I didn't want to be 'steady' or 'sensible' and I certainly didn't feel particularly nice. I felt bitter and vindictive and thoroughly selfish and if Simon was offering me a good time, I was going to have it, and on my terms, too.

We were on our way, belatedly, to the races. I'd only ever been once before when I was a child and my father had taken me to see the Derby. In those days my parents hadn't the money to risk gambling and after they had died, neither had I. I'd warned Simon I knew nothing about 'form' or 'tote doubles' or even how to place a bet but he'd seemed pleased with the idea of acting instructor to me and had been tolerant about our not arriving until the three o'clock race.

As we turned into the car park, I thought how pleasant it was to be taken out by someone who knew their way around so well and was sophisticated enough to be completely at ease in any surroundings.

Simon's mother might not be able to give him an allowance but he certainly must be earning a good salary whatever his job, for he pulled out a notecase full of ten pound notes and proceeded to bet in those denominations. I tried not to show my surprise, nor my concern when his horse was not even placed in the first race. To lose ten pounds in as many minutes seemed crazy to me. Simon looked unperturbed.

'I'm going to be lucky today, I know it!' he said, and doubled the stakes for the three-thirty. I refused to put more than a pound each way on my horse which I had chosen entirely because of its name, Harriet. I'd been only that morning typing a page of *The Crimson Tapestry* in which a Harriet Barclay featured. It was an outsider and hadn't, so Simon told me, a chance. However, it did come in second and although I was richer by only a few pounds, I could hardly contain my excitement. Simon seemed annoyed.

'When you have a hunch, you should always back it to the hilt,' he said. 'If I'd known why you picked it, I'd have put a tenner on for you.'

I told him I wouldn't have considered the winnings mine even if he had and he gave me a strange little look and said:

'No, I don't think you would. Funny girl. Doesn't money matter to you?'

'Of course!' I told him. 'But it's not the

most important thing in my life by any means. Happiness is my aim.'

Simon shrugged.

'Well, money can buy a hell of a lot of happiness,' he said. 'And it's damn near impossible to be happy without it. Oh, well, here goes!' He trebled his bet for the four-o'clock.

When the horses came bursting out of the starting gates and went thundering past us, I could hardly breathe. I had not bet myself but the thought of Simon's thirty pounds at stake made me feel slightly sick with apprehension. Beside me, he stood perfectly still and calm as if he stood to lose no more than thirty pence. But I ceased looking at him as the horses approached the winning post. I could make out the jockey in the blue silk shirt and cap whipping Simon's horse as it moved slowly but steadily ahead of the others. I think I must have been shouting myself hoarse as it thundered home, an un-disputed winner. A little embarrassed by my exuberance, I turned to apologise to Simon but I need not have worried – he was as excited as I. He caught me round the waist and hugged me to him.

'We've won! We've won!' he shouted. 'At twenty to one, Jennifer. Do you realise what that means, darling? Six hundred quid. It's all your doing. You're my good luck charm. I knew it. I just knew it.'

He kissed me hard on the lips and before I'd recovered, whisked me away from the stand to go and collect his winnings. I knew then that I had been mistaken in thinking Simon either calm or unconcerned when that race had started. He'd merely been holding himself in a tight control. Now that he had let go, he was like a child at Christmas – barely able to stop talking, laughing, rejoicing all at once.

By mutual agreement, we scrapped the rest of the races. Anything else would have seemed an anti-climax. Simon was all set for celebrating.

'We'll go wherever you like, Jennifer. Just name it. London? Paris, if you like. Let's do just that – get on an evening flight to Paris! Ever been there? It's a hell of a place to enjoy yourself if you know your way around. I'll show you, Jennifer. I'll take you to…'

'You're not really serious?' I broke in, realising that he was in fact meaning every word of it. 'If you are, the answer is quite definitely "no". Look at me! I indicated the rather unexciting cotton skirt and pale blue pullover I was wearing. 'And even if I was dressed by Mary Quant in whatever one wears at night in Paris, I couldn't go just like that!' I snapped my fingers.

'Why not?' Simon asked. 'Who's to stop you?'

'Well, your aunt, for one,' I answered. 'You keep forgetting I'm a working girl. And what's more, I wouldn't dream of asking her for time off. She's always been more than generous to me and I wouldn't take advantage of her.'

The laughter left Simon's face and for a moment he looked like a spoilt, sulky child. Obviously he wasn't accustomed to his girl friends pricking his bubbles. And equally obviously he was very much a creature of impulse. I couldn't think of anyone I'd ever met who would decide in the space of one minute that they wanted to fly to Paris and then be prepared to carry out the plan. I had little doubt that Simon would have taken me had I been willing. But I didn't let myself treat his invitation seriously. Of course I couldn't go. I wondered whether Simon would continue to sulk silently for the rest of the day, but again he surprised me. Only a few minutes later as we left the car park and drove towards Chichester, he turned and said in a perfectly normal voice:

'Just as well you called off, Jennifer. I'd clean forgotten I've a 'phone call coming through to the house this evening – rather an important one.'

For a moment his face looked strange. I wasn't sure if his expression was one of anxiety, worry or anger. Then he smiled and in his affectionate bantering tone, said:

'See what you do to me, Jennifer, luv! One look at you and all other thought flees my mind.'

As we drove slowly back to the Manor, I was as silent as Simon, lost in thought about him. It was strange the way one moment I felt I was beginning to know him very well and the next, felt a total stranger sitting beside someone quite unknown to me. Simon himself, was responsible, I decided – familiar as an old friend for half an hour and then suddenly withdrawing into a world from which I was obviously excluded. I found these switches of mood difficult to cope with. My own nature was a fairly simple one – or so I had always imagined until recently when overnight I found my-self acting unpredictably! But I was basically all for the security of the understood, the familiar, the explicable, the dependable. I wanted the fun without the danger!

As we turned off the main road we passed my cottage – the home Peter and I would never now share. I tried not to look at it but Simon said:

'I've a couple of American friends just over from the States who would give you a wonderful rent for that place, Jennifer. Now you've broken your engagement, are you considering letting it?'

I thought of Allan's request to rent it and my instant reaction was the same to Simon's question. I didn't want anyone living there. It was mine – mine and Peter's and...

I pulled myself up sharply. My thinking was ridiculous. We'd either got to sell the place or rent it. Either way, there would be strangers living there. I was in no position to disregard the financial situation. Peter and I were still meeting the regular mortgage repayments. We'd both had standing arrangements with our banks to pay the building society on a fifty-fifty basis. The quicker we were both relieved of this the better. I'd already telephoned the estate agent and asked him to look out for a buyer. But I knew that this had not committed me to anything. At the very back of my mind I still hoped Peter would come rushing back to England to tell me he couldn't live without me!

Fool! I told myself bitterly. All the time you were hoping, Peter's letter was on the way telling you there was no hope. Face up to it. There's another girl in his life now. Admit it!

But Simon had offered me a respite. I *could* rent the cottage on a short lease if the rent were high enough to meet the mortgage repayments plus any additional extras and supply a profit that would tempt Peter to agree to leasing rather than selling. Then, if his new romance burned itself out and he changed his mind...

My thoughts made me feel ashamed of myself. I ought to have more pride. But somehow, whilst not admitting it to anyone else in the world and most of the while not to myself either, I still wanted Peter; I'd forgive and forget if he gave me half a chance – if he came home and convinced me he really loved me.

'What kind of rent do you think your friends would pay?'

My voice sounded hard and mercenary but Simon did not appear to notice.

'I reckon you could pretty well name your own figure,' he said. 'They've got plenty!'

'But the cottage is only small,' I pointed out, 'and although it has "all mod cons", it's hardly the kind of place I'd have thought would interest rich Americans.'

'That's where you are wrong. They want a small weekend place – not a permanent residence. A sort of *pied à terre* but in the country instead of in London. It would suit them fine.'

Simon pulled the car to a halt outside the Manor and turned to look directly at me. His eyes had that same excited flash in them I was beginning to relate to moments when he very much wanted something. I said instinctively:

'Is it important to you, then, Simon?'

He looked away and gave a quick laugh.

'In a way, yes! They are ... business associates of mine. It would help me a lot, Jennifer, if I did them a good turn. You know how it is in business – tit-for-tat.'

'And are they nice people?'

He was no longer smiling.

'Well, not what you'd call nice. I suppose. You wouldn't want them as friends. But they are important – to me. Tit-for-tat again, luv. You help me by agreeing to have them as tenants and I'll help you by seeing you get a walloping good rent for the place. Is it a deal?'

I hesitated. Money wasn't all that important to me. But I couldn't disregard the fact that it was all-important to Peter. He'd want me to go ahead – that I was sure.

'I'd have to consult Peter,' I said slowly.

Simon put an arm round my shoulders and gave me a brief hug.

'That's my girl!' he said warmly. 'It's a shrewd move to make. With property rocketing in value every year, you'll make a good profit on what you paid for it. You could point that out to Peter, too.'

Simon was talking now as if it was a *fait accompli*. I felt suddenly unsure of myself without being able to find one reasonable argument against his suggestion. On the face of it why should I care who was in the cottage? I'd prefer they weren't people I liked, with whom I might become friendly. I didn't want to go near the place, let alone inside in where my heart would be tormented by every object; by the reminder of every broken dream.

'Send him a cable tonight!' Simon was saying. 'I'll stand the cost. The fact is they want somewhere urgently and they might not wait if they find somewhere else whilst you and the boy friend are exchanging letters. What about it, luv?'

The more he pressed me the more my

instinct was to back away, yet weakly I could not think of any valid reason not to cable Peter. In my heart I was certain his reply would be a brief 'Go ahead!' and the cable wasn't even necessary except that I would presumably need his written approval for the building society and the estate agent if I rented the cottage through them. But Simon seemed to think this was unnecessary.

'They'll only take a percentage of the rent – and for what, Jennifer?' he argued. 'They haven't found the tenants for you – I have! And then you'd be throwing part of your profit down the drain. A solicitor will draw up a lease according to your instructions. That will cover you. You don't need an estate agent.'

We went indoors and through to the dining-room where a cold supper was laid out ready for us. Simon proceeded to eat hungrily but I had no appetite. The wells of emotion that the thought of Peter had evoked in me, together with my own unaccountable feeling of apprehension, gave me a sensation of sickness and I only toyed with my food.

The telephone rang whilst we were still at the table and when Simon excused himself to rush off and answer it, I, too, left the room and went up to see Lady Barclay. As I climbed the stairs to our wing, I felt slightly guilty at having neglected her all day. It was a lonely life for her and I knew she liked having my company.

But I need not have worried. She was poring over her papers, her empty supper tray still unremoved beside her.

She smiled as I went towards her and like an excited child, called me over to her work table.

'Look, Jenny!' she said. 'I've discovered the answer to one of the missing links.'

She pointed to some notes she had written in her thin wavering and beautifully formed script.

'In the Domesday Book, the Barclay estate was recorded as being fifteen hundred acres, and included the church, the river and the mill. The mill, Jenny, was worth just over a sovereign!'

She gave me a delighted smile.

'And to think that the Mill House was sold last year for fifty thousand pounds! This house, Barclay Manor, was worth twenty pounds and later its value dropped to fifteen shillings. When you consider its worth today, those facts are quite incredible!'

I was caught up as always by her enthusiasm.

'A good example of inflation!' I quipped.

Lady Barclay laughed.

'I've been trying for the last two years to find out the size of the estate in those days!' she said. 'And to think that the information was there all the time, in the Doomsday Book! It must be old age, Jenny. Why, there may be dozens of other details relevant to the Barclay history in it. I want you to get to the library first thing tomorrow and find out how we can obtain a copy. I see in the encyclopedia that separate editions have been produced covering each county. There may even be a copy in the library now!'

I hated having to pour cold water on her enthusiasm but was forced to point out that tomorrow was Sunday.

She sighed.

'Then I'll just have to be patient until Monday. What a pity!'

To console her I reminded her that we had lots of time ahead of us to continue our research. But she gave me a strange look which seemed almost pitying.

'For you, Jenny, there is lots of time. But for me … well, there may not be enough that I can afford to waste a day.'

Her words filled me with foreboding.

I knelt down quickly by the side of her chair and grasped her hand.

'Don't say things like that, please!' I begged her. 'It's not true, anyway. You aren't *that* old!'

She smiled at my childishness.

'But I am, child!' she said gently. 'And to tell you the truth, Jenny dear, I have a very strange premonition that my time is limited. I must finish this book before I die. I must!' She seemed now to have forgotten me and to be talking to herself. 'If I don't complete it, who is there to do so? Thomas won't. Julia and Simon most certainly will not. There is no one … no one…'

'There's me!' I said fiercely. 'I would. You know I would. Maybe I couldn't do it as well as you but I'd try, even if it took me years and years.'

I was horrified to see tears glisten in those soft blue eyes.

'You really do care, don't you, Jenny? About *The Crimson Tapestry*, I mean?'

'Yes, I do,' I said truthfully. 'Not just because it means so much to you but because it fascinates me. I know I'm not "family" and it really is no concern of mine, but I feel involved.'

She patted my hand, her face relaxed and smiling again. We sat silently, feeling very close. After a minute or two, she said:

'Some people believe in reincarnation, Jenny. I do, and there are times when I've wondered about you – remember how like I thought you to Edwina Barclay. But that's just being fanciful ... the wish father to the thought. You see, dear, I would very much *like* to think you were part of this family. If Simon had been a Barclay I would have done everything I could to encourage you to marry him.'

'I'm very flattered!' I said genuinely. 'But there's nothing aristocratic about me, Lady Barclay. Nor has there ever been a title in my family.'

'Oh, my dear, there have been several Barclays who have married commoners!' Lady Barclay argued. 'But let's be thankful Simon has no connection for I would be sorely tempted to wish such a marriage on you, and that would scarcely be very kind to you, would it?'

I remained silent. I'd temporarily forgotten Lady Barclay's antipathy to Simon.

With uncanny intuition she said:

'Your silence is in itself a refutation of my remark. You aren't getting fond of the boy, are you, Jenny? If so, then stamp on such sentiment quickly, I beg you. He's not the right man for you in any event. You need someone to look after you, my dear.'

I refused to be drawn into a serious discussion. I said brightly:

'Why a minute ago you were telling me you'd have pushed me into marriage with Simon if he'd been a Barclay!'

She gave me a long, searching look and seemed on the point of argument. I felt oddly uncomfortable and rose from my kneeling position by her chair and went across to fiddle with her supper tray. I did not want to meet the look in her eyes or have her search so deeply into mine. It felt at times as if she knew my thoughts no matter how I tried to conceal them with words. But she said nothing and using the tray as an excuse to leave the room I told her I would take it down to the kitchen and out of her way.

She made no move to detain me and with a brief good night, I left her feeling once more in total emotional confusion. In a way, I loved the old lady. My close association with her had brought about a genuine respect and admiration for her so that I could not have felt more fond of her if she had been my own grandmother. But I resented her intrusion, however mild or brief, into my personal life. She had no right to dictate to me how I should feel towards Simon. If I wanted to like him I'd do so. If I wanted to go out with him I would go. If I wanted to be friendly with him what business of hers was it to try and put me off him? Moreover, if I wanted to marry him, which I did not, I'd do so without her permission.

I found myself at the foot of the great staircase boiled up with indignation that had no relation to the mild cautions my poor Lady Barclay had given me; especially since I had used her as a confidante whenever I'd wished in the past to talk about Peter. I'd really no justification for resenting her desire to question my feelings for Simon since I'd hardly been very reticent about my private life in the past. All the same, I didn't think she was being fair to Simon.

I felt even more strongly anxious to defend him when he joined me in the drawing-room as excited as a schoolboy with the news that he'd got his rich American friends to agree to the astonishing rent of a hundred pounds a week for my cottage.

'That's bound to mean a handsome profit

for you, luv!' he said, swinging me off my feet and round in a circle. 'How's that for a neat bit of negotiating?'

A hundred pounds a week sounded a fortune to me. And Simon had fixed this just to please me.

'They are driving down tomorrow to see the place,' Simon told me as he pulled me down on the sofa beside him. 'So you must get that cable off to your ex at once. But first, how about a kiss, my reward? You owe me one, don't you think?'

'I don't give kisses as rewards!' I said. 'I give them because I want to or not at all!'

But Simon obviously didn't intend to argue the point. His arms were drawing me towards him and his mouth closed over mine, stifling any protest I might have made. And within a minute, I no longer desired to make any. I was as hopelessly and helplessly lost in his embrace as a fly caught irrevocably in the spider's web.

Later, thinking back on that moment, I am not sure whether I had the strength of will left to resist Simon's demands. I would like to have believed so but I doubted it. Fortunately, when reason was about to desert me, the phone rang. At first Simon ignored it. Then swearing viciously, he got up to answer it. I had partially recovered my equilibrium when he returned. His face was white with anger.

'It's that bloody American!' he said, breathing deeply as if it was a struggle to keep from saying even worse. 'Wants to speak to you.'

Just for a moment I couldn't think to whom he was referring. My first thought was of his friends, the prospective tenants. Then I realised whom he meant and simultaneously, why he was so angry.

'Allan!' I said stupidly. 'What does he want?'

Simon gave me a long cold stare.

'You!' he said violently. 'He wants what I want, Jennifer – *you!*'

6

Human nature is a strange thing, I reflected, as I walked towards the telephone. There I was, still in love with Peter, violently attracted to Simon and yet still capable of being susceptible to the flattery of Allan's persistent efforts to be friends with me! I felt uneasy at my own instability.

I felt even further confused by the feeling of irritation when I discovered that Allan Howe had not rung me up to make a date as I had automatically assumed.

'I've some news for Lady Barclay, Jenny,' he told me as soon as I picked up the telephone receiver. 'I guess she's gone to bed but you could pass it on first thing in the morning. I'm not interrupting anything, am I? Simon didn't seem too sure whether you could come to the 'phone.'

I drew a deep breath, feeling an hysterical desire to laugh. But it wasn't really at all funny when I thought what, in fact, Allan's call had interrupted. How he'd despise me if he knew!

'That's okay!' I said vaguely. 'What's the news, then?'

Allan's normally slow, even drawl quickened with an excitement he was not troubling to conceal.

'I was in Bateley churchyard today,' he said, 'looking at the epitaphs on some of the old tombstones, and Jenny, I found all the Howe family were buried there. There was no tombstone for Edwin but he is mentioned on his parents' tombstone. Listen, Jenny.'

112

I heard the rustling of paper and then Allan's voice:

'*To the loving memory of Thomas and Elizabeth Howe, mourned by their children, Thomas, Hope, Matthew, Edwin and Matilda.*'

'Don't you see, Jenny? It proves that Edwin Howe came from this part of the world – right close by the Barclay family. And although there are other Howe tombstones for Thomas and Matthew, there is none for Edwin, which there wouldn't be if he died in America!'

Whether Allan Howe could prove his link with the Barclay family was really no concern at all of mine but nevertheless, I found myself vaguely stirred by this information. Perhaps it was just that I knew Lady Barclay would be so interested.

'I was wondering if it would be convenient for me to call on the old lady tomorrow,' Allan was saying. 'Would you ask her for me, Jenny? I sure would be grateful.'

I said I would pass on the request in the morning.

'Thanks, Jenny. You'll be around, I suppose? Maybe we could take Bramble for a walk in the woods afterwards. Would you be free?'

I was once again conscious of being

piqued. He'd thrown in the invitation as an afterthought!

'I'm sorry, but I won't!' I said. 'I've some people coming down to see over the cottage – the new tenants most probably.'

There was a moment of silence. Then I heard Allan's voice, hesitant and puzzled.

'I thought you were going to sell the cottage?'

'Well, I've changed my mind!' I replied sharply.

Another brief pause and then Allan said:

'That can't take all day – showing the tenants rounds, I mean. Will you have lunch with me, or dinner?'

Slightly mollified by his persistence, I said:

'I'm sorry, Allan, but I can't. Simon is down for the weekend and I'm more or less committed. I'm sorry!' I repeated.

'So am I! But I'm not giving up, Jenny. I'll ask you again next week – when Simon won't be there, I take it?'

'I'd like that,' I replied, ignoring the reference to Simon. 'See you then!' And I rang off.

Feeling thoroughly smug and self satisfied, I stood alone in the hall savouring the fact that despite Peter's rejection of me, I had two men in my life, both interested in me and jealous of each other. It was indeed balm to the wound. Perhaps Peter would feel a little jealous, too, if he knew that far from crying my eyes out for him I had a boy friend for weekday entertainment and another for the weekends!

But I couldn't stay on my pinnacle of vanity for long. Deep down inside me, I knew that I wasn't in the least in love with either Simon or Allan. It was Peter I wanted – the old, familiar love that had been part of my life so long I doubted I could ever disregard its importance to me. I wanted the man who didn't want me. If Peter came home to me, I wouldn't care if I never saw Simon or Allan again.

I looked up to see Simon standing silently in the doorway of the drawing-room, watching me. How long he had been there I didn't know. How much he guessed as to my feelings I couldn't know either. But he must have had some instinctive idea for he, too, was thinking of Peter.

'That cable to Peter!' he said. 'It ought to be sent off now.'

I nodded and with Simon still watching me, walked back across the hall to the 'phone.

Sunday dawned brilliantly warm and sunny. I woke with the memory of Simon's goodnight kiss on my lips and felt anew the now familiar stirring of excitement. We had the whole day to spend together – a beautiful Spring day. I wasn't going to let anything or anyone spoil it.

Nevertheless, it was spoilt. At breakfast I found a note from Simon saying he'd left early by car for London as he had decided it would be more agreeable to drive my 'prospective tenants' down to the Manor instead of meeting them off the train as I had gathered last night was his intention. *'Back soon after lunch'*, he ended.

I don't know why, but when Lady Barclay questioned me as to Simon's whereabouts and my own plans for the day, I deliberately withheld the facts. I suppose I knew instinctively that she would disapprove of any of Simon's friends renting my cottage since she had always written them off as 'a worthless crowd!' There would be time enough, I told myself, to cross this bridge when I knew it was there to cross. In the meanwhile, Simon's Americans might not like the place; they might consider the rent far too high for so insignificant a house; or Peter might reply to my cable with a demand to me to sell, not let it.

I had nothing to do all morning so I went out into the garden with Lady Barclay to help snip the dead heads off roses – a pastime she very much enjoyed and often did in the evenings when we'd completed our work for the day.

We were there together when Allan Howe turned up. I had completely forgotten about him and the message he had asked me to give Lady Barclay. As he came walking across the lawns towards us, guilt made me blush like some silly schoolgirl. I felt ashamed at my own selfishness and embarrassed knowing that in a matter of minutes, Lady Barclay would hear how forgetful I'd been.

The old lady went forward with a pleased smile on her face and spoke first.

'How very nice of you to call, Allan!' she said with real warmth in her voice. 'It is an unexpected pleasure!'

Allan shot me a quick questioning look. My face was still scarlet and obviously he guessed the truth. But he was nice enough not to betray me. He merely said:

'I came here because I have some information for you, Lady Barclay,' and he proceeded to tell her what he had told me the previous evening on the 'phone.

Lady Barclay turned to me with a brilliant smile.

'Did you hear that, Jenny dear? This is exciting, Allan. Jenny, do you realise we just might have another Barclay – an American one – standing here with us this minute!'

I was still speechless. Allan rescued me.

'It doesn't prove anything, of course,' he said. 'But it certainly does seem a remarkable coincidence that Edwin's should be the one tombstone missing when the rest of the Howe family are there. Of course, the girls in the family would no doubt have married and been buried with their husbands under other names.'

Lady Barclay nodded.

'And we can't ignore the fact that this Edwin could have fallen in battle somewhere far away – France, perhaps. In those days, people didn't have bodies brought home for burial.'

'Or he could have died in a prison, or drowned at sea!' Allan added. 'I've faced up to the fact that there probably are at least a dozen alternatives. But I intend to find out, Lady Barclay, just what did happen to him – if I can. I saw the Vicar this morning and he is going to look through the church records for me – see if he can discover whether the Howes were old Barclay retainers.'

Lady Barclay linked her arm through Allan's as if it were the most natural thing in the world. They walked ahead of me, slowly, towards the house.

'If this is the Edwin who ran off with Clarissa Barclay and Clarissa did come from our family,' Lady Barclay was saying, 'then we can be fairly sure the Howes lost their position with the Barclays when he did so. In those days, sons usually followed in their father's footsteps, so if your Edwin was a groom, his father was probably head groom and Edwin and his brothers would have begun as stable lads.'

I listened with half an ear, feeling excluded from their exchange of ideas. I did not follow them into the drawing-room where they were going to have a pre-lunch sherry, but went to my own room where I studied my reflection with dismay. I was wearing faded denim jeans and an old T-shirt and my hair was all over the place, tangled and messy-looking. I had begun automatically to tidy myself a bit when the thought occurred to me that Allan might imagine I was sprucing myself up for his benefit, so I pulled the T-shirt on again, ruffling my hair as I did so, and deliberately went downstairs looking my worst.

Allan gave me a cheerful grin as I came in and with his usual impeccable manners, stood up.

'Lady Barclay has very kindly insisted I stay for lunch,' he told me, pouring me a glass of sherry as if he were quite at home. 'I gather food had been ordered for Simon and as he isn't here to eat it, I'm more than welcome!'

I took the sherry glass with a bare nod of thanks. I was feeling resentful again, Allan was just too perfect. If old Lady Barclay was going to mistrust anyone it should be Allan Howe, not Simon. Why couldn't the old lady see that he was just ingratiating himself? This was the third time he'd succeeded in getting himself invited to a meal with us!

'Simon is coming back soon after lunch with some friends,' I said somewhat irrelevantly. 'So I'm afraid I won't be here to help entertain you this afternoon.'

'But that won't be necessary, Jenny,' Lady Barclay said. 'Allan and I are going to go through some letters together, so feel quite free, dear, to do whatever you've planned.'

I could feel Allan's eyes on me but I wouldn't meet them. I supposed he would be looking puzzled or hurt or annoyed. I went quickly over to the window and stared out into the garden.

At lunch I was unable to avoid being drawn into the conversation. Allan deliberately addressed questions to me, so that I could scarcely avoid answering without being obviously rude. The curtness of my replies did not seem to provoke him to silence and I reached the conclusion that he must have a hide like a rhinoceros not to have sensed by now my antagonism.

Lady Barclay, however, was well aware of my mood for eventually she came as near to a reproach as she had ever done, saying:

'Aren't you feeling very well, Jenny dear? You do sound a little out of sorts.'

I could see Allan's face break into a grin and I positively hated him in that moment. It seemed impossible that I could ever have thought him likeable. He had a knack of making me behave like an immature schoolgirl and I resented it. I said coldly:

'I'm probably tired. Simon and I were up pretty late last night!'

This time I knew that I had hit home. Lady Barclay looked distressed and Allan – I'm not sure what his expression revealed ... anger, perhaps? Jealousy? Whatever it was, it silenced him for he did not address another word to me for the rest of the meal. I was pointedly ignored. So that I would not appear to notice, I myself became very talkative, chattering away to Lady Barclay as if I hadn't seen her in weeks.

I slipped away before coffee was brought to the drawing-room and went up to my room to wait for Simon's return. I assumed he would bring his friends to the house and wanted to be able to greet them with a bit more sophistication than I'd greeted Allan earlier!

When Simon came, however, he was by himself. He gave me a quick but very personal kiss and then told me he'd dropped his friends at the cottage.

'Good thing, too,' he added. 'I see the old girl has visitors. No point getting messed up with a crowd when there's business to be done.'

'It's Allan,' I told him, following him out to the car. 'Didn't you recognise his Mini?'

Simon snorted.

'Blasted fellow always hanging round!' he muttered. 'Still trying to prove his connections to the English aristocracy?'

They had been my thoughts only an hour or two ago but now I suddenly found myself defending Allan.

'I don't think he's a snob!' I argued as we shot off down the drive, scattering gravel on to the grass verges in a way the old gardener must certainly have objected to if he'd been around to see.

'Well, I do. And I'll bet the Old Trout is encouraging him!'

I would have chided him for that horrible nickname but we were already drawing up by the cottage.

My first impression of Simon's friends was very far from favourable. I'd assumed they were a couple – man and wife, but in fact they were two men looking like the worst type of tourist – flashy, loud, thoroughly over-dressed for an afternoon in the country. They were too everything – too fat, too talkative, too brash, too much all over me with compliments and praise of the cottage. I judged them to be around forty in age but it was difficult to tell as it was a type I knew little about, except on films. I simply could not understand how Simon could call either of them 'friends'. Then I remembered that he had called them business associates and I found myself wondering, whilst they talked, what kind of business Simon could possibly have with them. The motor car trade seemed the most probable background.

My instinctive reaction was one of revulsion. Of all the people who might live here, in my dream home, these men were two I would least easily have considered. But I didn't see how I could go back on my promise now – and I had told Simon I'd rent it to his friends if Peter agreed. I'd not yet heard from Peter. Maybe there would be a last minute reprieve if he said 'Sell!' As we walked round the cottage, I began to hope more and more urgently that he would ask me to sell. I even toyed with the idea of telling Simon a lie if he told me to go ahead and let the cottage.

One of the men – the one Simon called Wilmer Reece, kept looking at me and winking at Simon in a way I can only describe as suggestive. His compliments, effusive and false, were littered with 'You're a swell kid', and 'You're quite a dish!' The other man, Holmer Deacon, was quieter but his smile was somehow worse than the other man's words. It was more a leer. We came out of the cottage into the sunshine and I hated them both.

Simon drew me to one side and put his arm around my shoulder. I was trembling.

'Look, Jennifer, don't be put off by

appearances. I know they're a pretty grue-some pair but they've got the money and that's what matters. And they'll pay.'

I felt sick.

Simon turned me round to face him and said slowly:

'It's natural you're upset. I don't blame you, Sweetie. I know how you felt about the cottage – the place you and that Peter of yours were going to share together … honey-moon house and all that. I do understand. But it's no good being sentimental at a time like this. In a way, it's better to have people living in it you don't give a damn about. Sort of writes off the whole episode. You mustn't be soft, luv. Look where sentiment got you – precisely nowhere. Just you leave it all to me. I'll fix everything for you and you needn't have anything more to do with them. Okay?'

I nodded. Until Peter's reply came I could do nothing so I was glad to escape from the company of the two men I'd taken such a strong dislike to. I left Simon to cope and walked slowly back towards the house.

Halfway along the drive, I saw Allan's car coming towards me. He stopped and leaned out of the open window.

'Lady Barclay has been looking for you, Jenny,' he told me. 'I think there was a tele-

125

gram for you from overseas.'

I felt my heart jolt. I could only mean Peter's cable.

'Shall I run you back to the house?'

I shook my head.

'It's okay, I'll walk!' I knew I sounded ungracious but I couldn't help it. Allan, however, opened the car door as if I hadn't refused the lift and waited for me to get in. Then he turned the car round and in silence drove me back up the long tree lined drive to the Manor. He didn't ask any questions or try to make conversation and I was grateful. But as I got out of the car, he put a hand on my arm and looked up at me and said:

'If you need me for anything, Jenny – anything at all – you know my number. Just telephone. Okay?'

I wanted to thank him but suddenly my throat felt choked. I was recalling that Allan had badly wanted to rent the cottage and I'd turned him down out of hand for no good reason at all. Yet in spite of my churlish, often rude behaviour, he was still offering me his friendship. Or was it his protection? Did I look as scared as I felt inside? And what was I frightened of? Simon's un-savoury friends? Peter's cable and what it might contain? It might read 'Don't rent or sell. I'm coming home.'

I stood staring back at Allan's calm open face in total confusion. All my life I had known my own mind; known what I wanted from life and how I intended to go about getting it. I'd known who I loved, who were my friends, who I liked, who I trusted. I knew exactly where I was going. Now, suddenly, my emotions were in total confusion and since I could not trust myself, who could I trust?

I looked down at Allan's hand, still lightly holding my forearm, warm, firm, undemanding, and knew that I wanted him after all as my friend.

7

The ensuing week did little to calm my bewilderment. The only certainty was Peter's brief reply telling me to go ahead and rent the cottage. *'Okay to rent, Peter.'* That was all – no personal message; not even 'Good luck' or 'Regards', let alone 'Love'.

'Saving money!' I told myself bitterly.

Disappointment would have made me an easy target for Simon had he been in one of his attentive moods. I was all set to go out somewhere with him on the Sunday evening and be every bit as 'mad' as he could be. I'd match him drink for drink, even go to Paris with him if he suggested it. I had no doubt that as soon as he'd seen his friends off on a train back to London, he would return to the house all set to go out and celebrate.

But apart from the briefest of minutes in which he informed me he was going to drive his friends back to town and would not be back himself until the following weekend, there was no sign whatever that he was, to use his own words of the previous evening, 'madly in love with me'. I was hurt, my pride severely piqued and yet at the same time I was relieved, knowing deep down that I was in a very vulnerable state of mind and heart and might all too easily have let Simon talk me into something I would have regretted later.

On Tuesday there was a totally unexpected letter for me from Julia. By this time I had mentally resigned myself to the fact that Simon did not seriously mean half the things he said and that I must accept that his attentions to me were not meant to be taken literally. Julia's letter confused me once more.

'I'm writing to invite you to come and stay with us in London for a week. I'm sure my sister-in-law would agree that you are due a holiday and should have a little more gaiety than she can hope to provide for you buried down there in the country. Simon is desperately anxious that you should be our guest. I am sure I have no need to tell you how deeply he cares for you, Jennifer, and I am so delighted that he has chosen such a very charming girl for his first serious love. I have never seen him so épris with any girl before and you will be made very welcome by us both.

I have written to Lady Barclay to beg her not to be selfish and keep you from the bright lights that any young girl of your age should be enjoying…'

'Well, Jenny dear, do you want to go?' Lady Barclay came straight to the point at breakfast as we read our letters. 'If you do, I shall of course allow you to do so. Julia is quite right – you have more than earned a holiday!'

I fingered Julia's letter uneasily. In a way, I did want to go. To go out dining and dancing, to the theatre, concerts, the ballet – to be escorted round London by Simon might be great fun. Yet the wording of Julia's letter almost made the invitation seem like a request for some kind of commitment from me. I felt instinctively that she was not just inviting me up there as she might have invited any other friend of Simon's but because she saw me as a possible future daughter-in-law! It was ridiculous, I told myself, to think of Simon in terms of marriage, yet that was what Julia's letter implied. I felt like writing back at once and telling her that I wasn't in the least serious about Simon and very much doubted if he was serious about me! I certainly did not want to go there on false pretences. I had no wish, either, to become involved with the 'smart young' set that Simon moved amongst in town.

'I see you are not sure!' Lady Barclay broke into my thoughts with her usual shrewd guess at the truth. 'You know the old proverb, Jenny. If in doubt, don't! I'm quite willing to write back to Julia and say I can't spare you.'

I did not need to ask her to be certain that *she* did not wish me to go. One thing I never doubted was her genuine affection for me and seeing how she felt about Simon, she would not willingly encourage me to further our friendship.

I told myself that to leave the old lady for a week when there was so much work on hand would be grossly unfair of me. It was, of course, an excuse for opting out of a situation that had somehow got out of control.

Accepting the fact of my cowardice, I let Lady Barclay take the blame for my refusal of the invitation.

On Thursday Lady Barclay asked me to telephone Allan and invite him to lunch.

'I've decided to offer him the old coach house to live in for the remainder of his visit to England,' she told me.

'But he's got accommodation!' I said without thinking. 'Why should you put yourself out for a complete stranger?'

It was none of my business and I had no justification for arguing against any decision she, my employer, chose to make. But the words were out before I remembered that fact.

'My dear Jenny,' she said quietly. 'Allan is not exactly a stranger, even if he is an American. He could very well be a distant relation!'

'That's ridiculous!' I lowered my tone of voice with an effort and said: 'There's no proof at all he's a Barclay. Besides, how do you know he'd even want to live here?'

'Because I made it my business to find out a little about him on his last visit to me. He's not at all well off, Jenny. He was telling me he found it hard to manage on his grant and he has no private means. The coach house flat has been empty since we dispensed with the chauffeur and I see no reason at all not to offer it to Allan. He can take his meals with us.'

I said nothing. Lady Barclay had obviously made up her mind and that was that – unless Allan refused. I had not thought about his financial means. I suppose I had just assumed that because he was an American, he had plenty of money! But I should have had some inkling because I knew the hotel he now lived in was anything but expensive. The fact that he had a car, however old and dilapidated, may have misled me, but now I knew his real circumstances, I could see that this would possibly be a cheaper form of transport than any other, especially as he could re-sell the car when he went back to the States.

Allan was out when I telephoned but he rang back during the afternoon when I was out walking with Bramble. When I returned at teatime, Lady Barclay informed me that Allan would be moving in at the weekend.

'I had a job to persuade him,' she told me, and added with relish: 'But I succeeded!' She chuckled mischievously. 'I told him that if he did turn out to be a Barclay, I'd feel so badly not having offered him hospitality that I'd never rest in my grave. So he's coming to please me. We must send old Anna across to clean the place thoroughly and it will need airing, too. I warned Allan it was furnished in the most spartan way but he says he doesn't mind in the least – bachelors don't bother about such things, do they? But you might go and see what you can do, dear, to make it look a little nicer once Anna has cleaned it. I do want him to be comfortable.'

As I went down to the kitchen to find Anna, the Polish woman who cooked and cleaned for us, I found myself wondering how Lady Barclay was going to react when she discovered Allan wasn't, after all, a family connection. She seemed to have it firmly fixed in her mind that he was. Either that or she had taken a very exceptional liking to him. But either way, he was a stranger and I was worried by her unquestioning trust. For all we actually knew, he could be the Boston Strangler! The old lady should at least have taken up references. We only had Allan's word for the fact that he was a university teacher.

In my heart, I didn't give much credit to my fears. Instinct told me Allan was totally trustworthy – incapable of deceit, let alone the possessor of evil intent! I was just trying to find reasons why he should not come to live at such close quarters. It might be more sensible, I decided, to question my own motives as to why I didn't want him living with us. Remembering the two rather unsavoury characters who were about to rent my cottage, barely a mile away, it might not be a bad thing to have a young strong male around the premises.

I forgot about Allan whilst I pondered again on the quandary I'd landed myself in. I had just not been strong enough to resist Simon's persuasions to let his friends have the cottage. But for Simon, I would most definitely have rejected them as tenants. But he had all but begged me, explaining that they were important business colleagues; that to disappoint them now they were so keen to have the place would be as detrimental to him as pleasing them would be advantageous. He did not explain why and evaded my questions, telling me I'd only be bored by the background to their business.

'You don't want to judge them on their appearances,' he told me convincingly. 'In any case, your solicitor will take up references for them when he draws up the contract. You've nothing to worry about, Jennifer, luv!'

It had become a habit now for Simon to telephone me every evening. The conversation always began with a plea to me to change my mind and accept Julia's invitation. It ended on a more personal note with Simon telling me he was counting the hours until the weekend when he would come down to see me.

'I'm crazy about you – I think of you all the time – I want you desperately! I can't wait to hold you in my arms again...'

I didn't feel happy listening to Simon making verbal love over the telephone. It wasn't that I feared Lady Barclay might be listening on the upstairs extension or that the lines might get crossed and someone else hear Simon's passionate demands. It was my own reluctance to face the fact that our relationship was such a physical one. I was very, very attracted by him but I didn't want to admit it to Simon or myself. If we went on this way, I might well find myself tempted to throw my morals to the wind and give Simon what he wanted. I was lonely, frustrated, and most relevant of all, rejected as a woman by the man I loved and had been going to marry. That Simon wanted me so desperately was a welcome balm to the still hurtful wound. It would be so easy to give way – to let myself live on a purely physical plane – yet to do so went against everything basic in my nature. Sex might fascinate me, for I was a perfectly normal young woman, but I had never been able to contemplate it without love. I didn't love Simon. I don't think he loved me. We were drawn to each other by a much more primeval stirring of the senses.

I worried about it – the more so because I could not completely forget that time in the beech woods when Allan had kissed me and I had found myself reacting to him, too. What kind of woman had I become that I could be responsive to any man who kissed me with passion? How could I possibly trust myself when I went around betraying everything I believed in? I preferred to forget that incident in the woods and the less I saw of Allan Howe, the easier it would be not to remember. Now I would be forced to see him every day at meals and each time I caught him staring at me in that thoughtful, contemplative way of his, I would be asking myself if he were wondering about that kiss, too.

But there was no going back. Lady Barclay meant to have Allan here at the Manor and the only way I could avoid him was to quit my job which I had no intention whatever of doing. Despite the emotional upheaval in my life, at least my interest in *The Crimson Tapestry* was consistent. I was very nearly as caught up in it as Lady Barclay herself. There were times when I was typing out her notes when I could barely restrain myself from adding phrases or descriptions of my own as if I, too, were a Barclay! I sometimes thought it wouldn't be so very difficult, were I a slightly more gullible person, to believe in Lady Barclay's theory of reincarnation. But I was realistic enough to appreciate that my deep interest in the Barclay family history was a very natural one. Not only were the people in it colourful and romantic, but their lives had been tremendously exciting and the book brought history, always one of my favourite subjects, beautifully to life.

How easy it was to picture the scene I had typed the day before ... young Charles

Barclay riding with Queen Elizabeth's entourage to stay at Cowdray Park in 1591...

'At breakfast three hundred oxen and a hundred and forty geese were devoured. On Monday, August 17th, Charles saw Her Majesty shoot three deer with her crossbow, the deer having been brought within range... On Wednesday accompanying the Queen to watch the fishermen drawing in their nets full of fish from a 'goodlie fish-pond'! On Thursday dining at table forty-eight yards long and enjoying a country dance with tabor and pipe. On Friday being knighted by her together with six other gentlemen before moving on to Chichester.'.

If I had been able to trace my ancestry back to 1591 it most certainly would not have revealed a member of my family in such illustrious settings.

The fascination of *The Crimson Tapestry* was endless. Lady Barclay actually had in her possession a letter from Sir Cedric Barclay written to his wife, warning her not to ride in St Leonard's Forest for *'a Headless Horseman named Powlett is said to ride there, not his Horse but Yours, seated on the Crupper with ghostly arms encircling your Waist.'*

No doubt the warning was taken seriously in those days.

Partly to please Lady Barclay but also from a sense of duty, I spent the Friday afternoon doing what I could to make the coach house flat as attractive as possible in readiness for Allan's arrival next day. I hung fresh cotton curtains in the small casement windows, put flowers in the little sitting-room and saw that there were adequate china, tea-pot, coffee-pot and other essentials in the kitchen. There was no bathroom and Allan would have to come across to the house for washing purposes but I presumed he knew this and did not object. At least the flat had been wired electrically, and there was an electric kettle with which he could boil water for shaving or tea.

When I had completed my task to my satisfaction, I felt quite proud of my efforts. The place really made extremely nice if simple, guest quarters. Lady Barclay came across to inspect and was delighted.

'You really do have a flair for home-making,' she told me smiling. 'Ever since you've been living with me, I've so admired the way you do the flowers. Now I can see that you have an all round artistic touch which will stand you in good stead, my dear, when you have your own home one day.'

This was my opening to tell Lady Barclay about my tenants for the cottage. I opened my mouth, intending to do so but somehow I just could not bring myself to speak. It was sheer funk. I was only too well aware that she would disapprove of any of Simon's friends living there, let alone the two disreputable-looking strangers I was convinced even Simon himself did not like. I deeply regretted my acquiescence and decided then and there that I would tell Simon so when he came down the following day and see if it was not too late to get out of the commitment.

So with this reassurance to myself that there was little point in worrying Lady Barclay over an issue that might never arise, I said nothing and stood silently watching whilst she pottered slowly around Allan's flat murmuring reminiscences of some past coachmen who'd lived there when she was a girl. Barclay Manor abounded with servants of all kinds in those affluent days – as many outdoors as indoors. The stables were full of horses – Lady Barclay and her brother each having their own riding pony and a little grey pony to draw the governess cart in which they were driven to and from the weekly dancing class they attended in Chichester.

As a rule I loved to listen to the old lady's stories of her childhood here, but this morning I felt restless and unable to concentrate. I think she sensed my feelings for she told me to go off for a nice long walk and enjoy the sunshine.

'Bramble needs some exercise!' she said. 'He's getting fat!'

Lady Barclay was devoted to Bramble. He was originally old Lord Barclay's dog, kept for the occasional weekends when he still came down to the Manor and liked to go rough shooting. But that was a long time ago. He had certainly not been down during my months of employment and I knew from Lady Barclay that for years now, his visits had been practically non-existent. He came about twice a year to see to the business side of the estate; pay his sister a short call and then disappeared up to London again. So Bramble, with a spaniel's devotion, had attached himself to Lady Barclay and although the old girl pretended she objected strongly to the dirt he brought into her house on his long silky coat and complained that he was quite undisciplined, she was as devoted to him as he to her. One of the terms of my employment was that I should be willing to exercise the dog! In fact I enjoyed our long rambling walks and felt quite pleased that Bramble, who was a one-woman dog, had come to accept me as a friend. I had rather neglected him of late – mainly because I'd been spending my free time at weekends with Simon and he, for some strange reason, positively disliked the poor old dog.

'Moults all over the chairs and ruins my clothes!' Simon had complained. 'I loathe the way spaniels always fawn over you!'

In fact Bramble did not fawn, unlike most spaniels, who were inclined to be sloppy. It was true he moulted badly in the spring and Simon was incredibly particular about his 'clobber' as he called his various outfits. He obviously took pride in looking fashionable and impeccably groomed and I suppose it was annoying to have long black and white dog's hairs clinging to his trousers. Nevertheless, I still felt guilty every time Simon pushed the old dog none too gently out of any room he happened to be in, saying:

'Let the Old Trout have his company!'

I did not seem able to stop Simon using this very unattractive description. He knew I disliked it and softened the words with a grin but I was not disarmed. I hoped, in time, to break him of it. Now that he was seeing so much more of Lady Barclay, it was my sincere hope that they would begin to like each other better. So far, I had not made much impression on either of them. I meant to try again this weekend.

Simon, however, was in no mood to feel kindly towards anyone – even me. When he arrived on Saturday morning, it was simultaneously with Allan who was carrying his suitcases across the drive to the courtyard in the process of moving in.

Simon got out of his car, his face all too revealing of his feelings as I explained Allan's movements.

'What the hell's right has he got to muscle in here!' he said violently. 'Has the Old Trout gone clean out of her mind? Why didn't you stop her, Jenny? Are you crazy too? We don't want a bloody p.g. falling about all over the house. He's here often enough as it is – far too often in my view…'

I waited until he stopped talking and then tried to point out that Lady Barclay's whims were no concern of mine and that the Manor was her house, to arrange as she wished.

It was not very tactful. Simon's face whitened and for a moment I was frightened of the violence in his eyes.

'That's right, rub it in that I've no rights here – nothing but an interloper in my own home. Well, I am a Barclay, whether my stepfather wishes to acknowledge the fact or not. I've got some rights, God damn it. I'll telephone my mother. I'm damned if I'm going to have that American stuffed down my throat. He can get out – the sooner the better. I'll get the Old Trout certified. She must be out of her mind!'

I prayed silently that Allan would not reappear until Simon had calmed down a bit. It had never occurred to me that he would react like this. I wondered if Lady Barclay had thought of it and if I should warn her. Yet none of it was my business. This was a family matter and I was not part of the family. In a way, I could see why Simon was reacting in such an extreme fashion. He obviously had an obsession about his relationship with the Barclays. As a stepson he had no rights and in view of his past, his stepfather had made it painfully clear that he didn't want anything to do with Simon. Nor so it seemed, did Lady Barclay look upon him as a nephew. His position, which might have been a magnificent one as the Barclay son and heir, was in fact, little better than a stranger's. And here was his aunt welcoming a total stranger in a way she had never welcomed him!

I all but pulled him after me into the dining-room and watched him down a brandy-and-soda anxiously. I hoped the strong drink might steady him and put him in a better mood before lunch. It did swing his attention away from Allan – to me.

'Good God, Jennifer!' he said, staring at me. 'You're more attractive than ever. Each time I see you you seem to have added a new dimension. Must be that tan. Come here. I want to kiss you.'

I went willingly enough into his arms, pleased not only that he found me attractive but that I had diverted him. He was even less restrained than usual and I tried to draw away from him as the tension between us mounted to a new fever.

'No, Jennifer. I'll not let you go. You're mine, do you hear? I want you. I'm going to have you. If I never have anything else, I'll have you...'

I began struggling to free myself. The grip of his fingers on my bare arms hurt me and whilst this was strangely exciting, I was also frightened. There was something in Simon's eyes, in his voice, in his bodily tension that I found unnerving.

'Please let me go!' I begged. 'Please, Simon, I...'

'Let her go!'

The words were like a gun shot, short, sharp, loud and totally unexpected.

Simon's grip on me fell away and we both swung round, staring stupidly at the man who had come unheard into the room. I caught my breath and with the inanity of absolute embarrassment, said:

'Oh. Allan. Come and have a drink!'

I heard Simon's quick intake of breath and then Allan's quiet, calm voice speaking as if nothing had happened:

'Thanks a lot. I will!'

8

It was Lady Barclay, following close behind Allan, who was inadvertently responsible for preventing the scene which I have no doubt at all was on the point of developing. I both sensed the violent muscular tension of Simon's body, only an inch or so from mine, and heard his quick indrawn breath as he was about to explode verbally at Allan's interruption.

'Well, isn't this nice!' Lady Barclay said in her tiny innocent bird-like tones. 'We're quite a little party. Would you pour me a sherry, please, Simon. Just a small one. And you, Allan. Have you settled in quite comfortably?'

The three of us unfroze from our statuelike immobility. Simon, after one quick furious look at Allan, turned away towards the sideboard to lift the sherry decanter. Allan's face broke into a smile as he expressed his pleasure in the flat.

'Oh, you must thank Jenny for the trimmings!' Lady Barclay said, meaning well but throwing petrol on the flames of Simon's resentment. 'She spent the whole of yesterday afternoon making the place nice for you, Allan.'

I blushed, hating everyone, Lady Barclay included, as I did so. But there was no escape for me. My cheeks flaming, I had to stand there and at least try to seem gracious as I accepted Allan's thanks. Churlishly, in the face of the genuine warmth of his words, I said:

'I was obeying Lady Barclay's orders!'

I hoped Simon as well as Allan took my

point – that I had made the effort not for Allan but for my employer. I could not help but see the smile vanish from Allan's face and the hurt look which replaced the pleasure that had been there. I felt mean and turned away to find Simon's eyes smiling at me in a kind of triumph. I felt even worse. I hadn't meant to score off Allan to please Simon.

'I must go and tidy up for lunch!' I excused myself angrily. Let the three of them sort themselves out. I was not going to let them involve me!

Lunch served today in the dining-room instead of in our private wing, was not to be avoided. Simon seemed to have recovered his composure entirely and to derive a measure of sadistic excitement from remarks made across the table to Allan that could be taken two ways – insulting, as he intended, or harmless as he wished Lady Barclay to understand them … remarks such as:

'What a fantastic change it would make in your life, Howe, if you turned out to be one of the illustrious Barclays after all! I expect you know there isn't an heir. Who knows but you could even prove your connections sufficiently to satisfy the legal wallahs that you should inherit not just the title and the

Manor but the Barclay fortune as well. How exciting that would be!'

I saw Allan's face go a dull red. But he spoke quietly:

'That isn't, of course, my objective. I am interested merely in tracing my family origins in this country. My future is already rooted in my own country, so I have no interest in the estate.'

'But Simon may be right!' Lady Barclay said happily. 'If you were a relation, no matter how distant, you could well turn out to have a legitimate claim to the title and the estate when my brother dies.'

'And what a happy ending that would make for your book, dear Aunt!'

Lady Barclay peered over her spectacles at Simon but meeting only an innocent smile, nodded happily.

'It would be quite perfect – in fact, I've not been able to put the thought out of my mind. Not that there is much of a fortune left to inherit, Allan. Death duties and taxation and the high cost of running the estate has reduced our family to near penury.'

'Oh, come, come!' Simon broke in with a sideways glance at Allan. 'Your illustrious brother, my honourable stepfather, hardly lives on a shoe string, does he? And I happen to know from my mother that he never touches capital. So his income must derive from a fairly large source, wouldn't you say? Nor is he ungenerous to my mother. No, I don't think I'd call this family penniless – not quite!'

I could see Lady Barclay was uneasy. Money was not a subject she liked to hear discussed at table, she told Simon. What were we young things going to do with our afternoon?

'I'm taking Jennifer to Chichester,' said Simon without consulting me. 'We'll leave you and Allan in peace to continue your machinations into the past. I'm sure Jennifer needs a change of air. A girl of her age must get fed up digging in the archives.'

At any other time I might have protested, for I really did love my work, but I decided Simon was in no mood to be thwarted. The best way to ensure that he was not jealous of Allan was to show him just how little Allan meant to me. Any excuse I made to stay at home would only seem to Simon an excuse to stay with Allan and that was the last thing I wanted either of them to think.

But we were not destined to go after all. Lady Barclay tripped over an upturned corner of one of the Persian rugs in the hall as we went through to the drawing-room for coffee; and whilst she was not really hurt at all, Allan suggested I should call the doctor because of the shock for anyone of Lady Barclay's age.

By the time I had put her to bed and the doctor had called I had put any idea of going out with Simon from my mind. Lady Barclay was dozing from the sedative the doctor had given her but I simply could not bring myself to leave her, even though Allan offered to sit with her.

'You go off with Simon if you want to, Jenny,' he said as we stood at the top of the staircase to our wing of the house, talking in whispers so as not to disturb her. 'I've nothing whatever to do and I can sit in your study and listen in case she needs anything. I'm really quite a dab hand with sick people!'

But it did not seem right to leave her – there were, after all, some things Allan could not do for her, and I shook my head.

'Well, at least go out for a bit – you could both take Bramble for a walk.'

He seemed very anxious to get rid of me but again I shook my head.

'Simon doesn't like walking. Besides, I intend to stay with Lady Barclay. It's my job to look after her.'

151

Allan nodded.

'Then perhaps I can sit with you?'

'Haven't you anything else to do?' I asked, more rudely than I intended. I was worried about Lady Barclay and uneasy at the way Simon would react. He was waiting impatiently downstairs and had already told me that I was making a mountain out of a molehill – he'd spoken to the doctor himself and been told there wasn't so much as a minor sprain to worry about.

Maybe Allan's meekness up to now had given me the wrong impression of him. I was certainly surprised when he rounded on me with a harshness I'd not encountered so far.

'I know you and Simon both resent my coming to live here,' he said icily, 'and I'd like you to know that my one and only reason for accepting Lady Barclay's invitation was because she had so set her heart on it that I didn't have the boorishness to refuse. Now, since I am here and since you profess to be so attached to her, at least let us try to get along. I've no quarrel with you, nor do I see why you should have any quarrel with me.'

The fairness of his accusation made me feel guilty but I was unwilling to apologise.

Instead, I said with equal coldness:

'I've certainly no wish to quarrel. What you do is your business and what I do is mine. Just leave me alone, that's all.'

I flung off in the direction of my own bedroom and threw myself down on the bed. I knew I'd behaved childishly. Allan had been the soul of helpfulness when the old lady had fallen. I ought to have been grateful. But at the same time, I resented the fact that he seemed to be continually making me feel obliged to him in some way; forced to like him. I think I'd have liked him better if he'd just had one thing wrong with him! I wanted to forget about him but he seemed always to be appearing at my elbows or bringing himself to mind in some unexpected way. If he'd just leave me alone!

I couldn't stay in my room avoiding Simon, too. I finally got up off my bed, tidied my hair and went downstairs to find him. He was out in the garden, lounging in a deckchair, his face sullen and angry.

'Bet the Old Trout did it on purpose!' he said scowling. 'And don't laugh, Jennifer. It isn't in the least funny – every time I make plans to be with you, something crops up to interfere. I'm fed up. I've a bloody good mind to go back to London!'

'All right, go then!' I challenged him.

He reached up and pulled me down into his arms.

'Not unless you come with me, Jennifer...'

I pulled myself quickly away. The urgency in his voice was a warning. I couldn't cope now with a fight for my honour! Trying to keep the atmosphere light-hearted I told him so.

'Honour!' Simon said disgustedly. 'Quaint old fashioned word that went out with the dodo. I suppose you'll cling to it to the bitter end and extract your pound of flesh.'

He saw my bewilderment and laughed scornfully.

'Oh, you're one of the ones who expect marriage before the marriage bed. I know your sort, Jennifer. Met a dozen like you. You use your virginity as your trump card.'

I turned away furiously but he caught my arm and held it.

'Don't be angry. I can't help it. You drive me wild. I want you. God damn it, I'll even marry you if I have to. You should be sorry for me, not angry. Where are you running away to now? To tease your other boy friend?'

I slapped him hard across the face. He'd picked the wrong moment to provoke me and he'd gone too far. But he wasn't annoyed. He laughed and kept his grip on my arm.

'A woman of fire and passion, my Jenny. Do it again, love, and see what happens. I find it quite exciting!'

There was a strange glitter in his eyes that frightened me. I felt instinctively that Simon was capable of trying to force himself on me. I was playing with fire!

'Please let me go. You're hurting me!' I said quietly. 'I don't like you like this, Simon.'

'Don't you?' He laughed without humour. 'Well, don't tease me, then. I never could stand being teased.'

His grip on my arm ceased but he caught my hand before I could draw it away and bit my thumb so hard that I cried out. Then he pushed my arm back against my side and rolled over on his side, his back towards me saying:

'Well, go and waste your lovely young life elsewhere. See if I care!'

I walked back into the house struggling against angry tears. None of this was my fault. I hadn't pushed poor Lady Barclay over the carpet! I hadn't asked Allan Howe to live in the flat. I hadn't wanted to spoil Simon's day, or my own. I seemed unable to please anybody, even myself!

9

I don't know what time it was when that night, on the point of falling asleep, I was roused by a knock on my bedroom door. I had no doubt in my mind that it was Simon and I held my breath waiting to see if he would knock again. He had not appeared at supper and I had assumed that he meant me to realise that he was thoroughly annoyed with me and intended me to see that he wasn't going to be pushed around by any girl. My emotions were mixed. Half of me reacted with an 'I don't care' attitude, yet the other half was piqued that he took a rebuff so easily. If he'd really cared anything for me he'd have tried to understand my feelings of obligation towards the old lady. He was just a spoilt boy wanting his own way. My difficulty was that I had been secretly looking forward to an evening with him. It was a beautiful night, the soft Spring air filled with the daytime scents of blossom and hyacinths and fresh mown grass. With the night had come a brilliant quarter moon and I found it impossible not to feel romantic. It would have been lovely to go for a drive with Simon, feeling the soft wind in my hair and the excitement of his closeness.

Now I was afraid to open my door. I wanted him to come in, sit on my bed, hold me in his arms and kiss me and tell me I was the most attractive girl in the world. Yet I knew it would not end there. Simon was not capable of a tender, restrained passion. So when the knock was repeated, I stayed silent, hoping that he would assume I was asleep and go away.

I caught my breath as the door opened and a male voice called my name.

'Jenny, wake up. It's me ... Allan. Jenny, are you there?'

I was too surprised to dissemble.

'It's *you!*' I said stupidly. 'I thought it was Simon!'

The next moment I was grateful for the darkness to hide my burning cheeks. Whatever must Allan be thinking after a remark like that? Obviously the worst for his voice was harsh and tense as he said:

'Sorry to disappoint you. I'm afraid the boyfriend is in a bad way. That's why I'm here. I need your help.'

'What's wrong?' I asked, leaning over and switching on the bedside lamp with shaking fingers. The room sprang to life and I could see Allan standing in the doorway, the frown on his forehead giving way to a faint look of bewilderment as he stared back at me. With total irrelevance he said: 'I don't understand you. I don't understand you!'

'And I don't understand anything!' I said, pulling my dressing gown over my transparent nylon nightie. 'You're just not making sense, Allan.'

He pulled himself together with a quite discernible effort. In the same harsh tone he had used earlier, he said:

'Simon's high. I need help to get him to his room.'

'High?'

Allan's eyes softened along with his voice.

'Drugged,' he explained. 'I'm sorry to involve you, Jenny, but he just won't budge for me. He's sitting on the landing outside Lady Barclay's room and I don't want her coming out and finding him like that. It would be a terrible shock.'

I was out of bed now, searching for my bedroom slippers. Allan came across and knelt down to search under the bed for me. Presently he found them and put them on my feet. I couldn't think clearly and he must have realised my bewilderment for he said:

'I'm sorry if I startled you. You look half asleep. Didn't you know Simon took drugs?'

I shook my head.

'Are you sure?' I asked stupidly. 'I mean, perhaps he's just tight and...'

'He's on drugs!' Allan interrupted harshly. 'I've seen enough of it in the States to recognise an addict. I knew the first time I met him. Naturally I assumed you knew too.'

'How could I?' I replied. 'I wouldn't know what to look for since I've never mixed with drug addicts.' The conversation seemed suddenly so unreal and so unbelievable that I added: 'And I don't believe Simon is an addict, either. I think you just don't like him and want to believe the worst of him and make me think the worst, too.'

'Jenny, grow up, please!'

There was reproof and yet a gentleness in Allan's voice that irritated me.

'The way you talk you'd think I was a child!' I said indignantly. His smile further infuriated me.

'I wouldn't if you stopped behaving like one! It's obvious you think I'm jealous of Simon. Well, let's clear that one up right away. I could only be jealous of someone I thought stood a better chance than I with the girl I wanted. Oh, he's attractive and I could quite see that you found him so – but you'd never *marry* a guy like that and that's all I care about. You see, one day, you're going to marry me.'

'And whatever gave you that idea?' I replied furiously. 'If ever there was a conceited, self opinionated, egotistical...'

'Honey, you and I have to go deal with the boyfriend!' Allan broke in grinning in a way that made me want to hit him. 'Otherwise I'd take up the cudgels with you on the matter of my character. Furthermore, however black my character, at least I have some morals.' The smile had left his face now and it looked close and bitter. 'Apparently you do not!'

'My morals have nothing whatever to do with you!' I shouted back at him. 'And what's more...'

'They do have to do with me!' he interrupted. 'You're the girl I'm going to marry. I don't want to share our marriage bed with Simon's memory.'

I was now quite out of control and I slapped him hard. Had he given any kind of reaction I think I would have slapped him again but he just stood there, looking at me with a terrible pained expression and then said:

'I'm sorry, Jenny. I deserved that. Please forgive me. I just couldn't stand the thought of ... of...' he broke off and walked away from me to the door, his face averted. I was trembling ... still angry and yet deep down inside, understanding. He really had believed I'd been going to let Simon into my bedroom – into my bed.

'If you think those sort of things about me how can you say you want to marry me?' I asked, not without bitterness. Yet I knew I could not claim total innocence. I'd wanted Simon – badly. I'd even hoped it would be he knocking to come in. Would I have said 'No'? If he'd insisted, would I really have refused?

'Forget I spoke!' Allan said from the door. 'I had no right and it was extremely rude and silly of me. I apologise. And now, if you're ready, we'll go down and deal with Simon.'

I was not at all sure what 'dealing' with Simon meant. I was to find out. The young man leaning against the wall outside Lady Barclay's room was not the Simon I knew, but a total stranger, living in a world of his own. Trying to reach him was like trying to talk to a mental defective – he simply didn't hear what Allan or I said.

I shivered, trying not to let Allan see how frightened I was. I'd read about 'trips' taken by consumers of LSD. Now I was seeing someone I knew in this state and I wanted to run away, not to see or hear what my senses were having to accept.

'We'll have to carry him to his room!' Allan said, calm and matter of fact in a world that seemed to be turning upside down all of a sudden. 'You take his feet ... I'll try to take most of the weight.'

'The spare room is nearer than his own room,' I told Allan. 'Just along the passage, second on the left. If we go to his room, we'll have to go downstairs and up the other staircase to his wing.'

Allan nodded.

'Spare room it is then. Is there a key to the door?'

I didn't know but fortunately we found one in the door and Allan locked it firmly behind us as we left.

'I'll let him out in the morning,' he said, more to himself than to me.

'Oughtn't we to call the doctor?' I asked.

Allan shrugged.

'It's not our business, Jenny. Simon's an adult. I'll speak to him of course, in the morning. Not that it'll do much good. I can only threaten to tip off the police that he has access to drugs. He's probably too canny to keep much of the stuff on him.'

'His mother?' I suggested. 'Ought we to warn her?'

'If he lives with her she probably knows!' Allan said wryly. Suddenly Julia's letter to me made sense. Of course she knew. Simon's 'set' probably all took drugs of one kind or another. That was why she welcomed me as his girl friend ... someone who might be able to break him of the habit, if habit it was. It hit me suddenly that Simon's strange changes of mood could now be explained. Morose, sulky, down one minute and up the next; his instability had been part of his attraction for me. I shivered and Allan must have noticed for he said:

'Come on. We'll go down to the kitchen and make some hot coffee.'

I did not argue, suddenly overcome with an enormous feeling of relief that Allan had been there to cope. What would I have done if I'd been alone in the house with only old Lady Barclay to help me? Suddenly I was struck with the realisation that Allan had been here in the house in the middle of the night.

Why?

I asked him but he refused to tell me until we were sitting either side of the kitchen table, hands cupped around steaming mugs of coffee.

'It's really quite simple,' Allan said at last. 'I noticed Simon's behaviour at dinner – you were sharing a tray with Lady Barclay, remember? He and I were alone. He was desperately on edge and I had a pretty shrewd idea he'd given himself a shot. I didn't like the idea of you two alone here with a sick old woman, so I hung around in the library knowing Simon would have to pass the door on his way up to his room. When midnight came and he still had not appeared, I made a search – and found him in that passage.'

'But why did he go there?' I asked stupidly.

Allan shrugged.

'Maybe hoping you would be around. I don't know. I just know it isn't safe for you to be in this house alone with him. It's one of the reasons I jumped at Lady Barclay's suggestion I should rent the coach house.'

'And I thought...' I broke off, the colour rushing to my face as I recalled the doubts I had about Allan – accusing him of trying to

164

ingratiate himself with the Barclays. I felt terrible and began an apology but Allan wouldn't let me make it.

'You weren't to know,' he said. 'Besides, it was possibly partly my own fault for not giving you my reasons. I was afraid you'd think I was trying to put you off Simon for ... well, for personal reasons.'

I looked quickly away, the expression in his eyes making me strangely uncomfortable. Allan had an uncanny way of guessing my reactions – I would have defended Simon and on the grounds Allan suggested – that he was jealous. What a conceited idiot I'd been. How he must be laughing at my gaucherie. I felt a little sick and not a little ashamed.

As if sensing my feelings yet again, Allan covered my hand with his and said gently:

'I know you don't even like me very much, Jenny, but I wish you'd at least *try* to do so. Just every once in a while I get the feeling that you could like me if you'd only let yourself. What are you afraid of? I've tried to puzzle it out but it doesn't add up. I should have thought Simon's type would have scared you more than I?'

'I'm not frightened of either of you!' I said vehemently, but the same thought must

165

have gone through Allan's mind as went through mine – 'methinks thou dost protest too much'! Well, maybe my statement wasn't altogether true. I was certainly scared of Simon now I knew more about him. But Allan ... why should I be frightened of him?

'Well, can't we be friends? Real friends?' Allan broke in on my thoughts. 'That's all I'm asking, Jenny. You must be lonely living here with only Lady B for company. I'm certainly lonely. We could have a good time together if you'd only stop avoiding me.'

Every word he said was true and in a way I did want to be friends. Yet...

'You see, Jenny? Even now you don't trust me. I wish I understood why!'

So did I. Simple though he seemed in one way, Allan confused me. I'd almost forgotten but now I recalled the incredible conversation we'd had earlier in my bedroom. He'd said I was the girl he intended to marry! Well, either he was crazy or I was. One didn't talk in terms of marriage one moment and friendship the next. Maybe he hadn't meant it. I didn't see how we could be friends if we couldn't communicate and I wasn't going to broach the subject. I'd made enough of a fool of myself with Allan without wishing to repeat the process.

'There are times, Jenny, when you look twelve years old!' Allan said. 'At others, you are all woman. I owe you an apology and now seems as good a time as any to make it. Up in your room a while back I implied that you and Simon...' he broke off and I filled the gap for him in a small harsh voice. 'Were lovers?'

He nodded, avoiding my eyes.

'Yes! You slapped my face and I deserved it.'

'Not altogether!' I said in a near whisper. 'I'm ... I'm not all that innocent – in thought, anyway. Simon attracted me.'

Allan nodded again as if this were the most natural thing in the world for me to be admitting.

'That I understand,' he said quietly. 'But he's not right for you, Jenny. I think you know that deep down. You aren't really in love with him, are you?'

'Good heavens, no!' I said truthfully. 'If it's love we're talking about, then I'm not in love with anyone and most certainly don't intend to be. I'm finished with love.'

Allan was looking at me with an expression I could not fathom.

'Still carrying a torch for Peter,' he said,

more to himself than me.

'I'm not. I hate him. He's made a mockery of everything I believed him to be. He betrayed me – and our love. I just hope I never have to set eyes on him again.'

Allan sighed.

'I wish you didn't hate him quite so vehemently!' he said. 'Hate's a near thing to love. Was he really worth it, Jenny?'

I felt suddenly near to tears. Was Peter worth all those years of devotion? What was he really like as a person? Did I know him at all? I couldn't see him objectively. He was just Peter, the boy I'd always loved. I wouldn't have fallen in love with him if I hadn't thought him worth it. Was Allan right and my hate really just another expression of the love I could not seem to eject from my system?

'Maybe you both just grew up and away from each other,' Allan said softly. 'It can happen when one falls in love at a very young age. Or perhaps the engagement dragged on too long.'

'Or if we'd lived together...'

'No!' Allan said firmly. 'I'm no Puritan, heaven knows, but I don't think sex ever cements a shaky foundation. I believe that kind of relationship puts the emphasis on the wrong things. For two people to get along well in bed doesn't guarantee they'll get along well out of it. So don't ever torment yourself with the thought that you might have kept your Peter if you'd agreed to sleep with him.'

'He never asked me to do so!' I defended Peter. 'We just never talked about sex.'

Allan eyebrows were raised in disbelief.

'In this day and age? I thought England was supposed to be The Permissive Society and Sex No. 1 topic of conversation for the young.'

I smiled in spite of myself.

'Well, don't believe everything you read in the papers. There are still lots of girls left with romantic ideals and boys like Peter who respect our feelings.'

Allan grinned.

'I'm glad to hear you are still a romantic, Jenny, despite that earlier oh-so-bitter remark about being finished for ever with love! Maybe there's hope after all that you'll fall in love with me. I do mean to marry you one day, you know.'

'Please don't say things like that, Allan!' I begged him, half smiling, half seriously. 'I know you don't mean it and that you're probably just trying to be nice – give my ego a boost or something. But I'd really rather you didn't tease or joke about it.'

'I wasn't teasing, or joking, or trying to boost your ego,' Allan said quietly. 'But I won't talk about it if the thought upsets you. I'll settle for your friendship for the time being, Jenny. Will you give it to me? That means I want your liking, your trust, your company. You don't *dislike* me, do you?'

'No, of course not!' I said, sure of least of this. 'And I think it's very noble of you even to want my friendship after the way I've behaved. I suppose I do badly need a friend – especially now Simon...'

I broke off, unwilling to put into words my complete reversal of feeling for Simon. I was sorry for him but I didn't think I could ever feel attracted to him again now I knew so much more about him. No wonder Lady Barclay had tried to warn me off him. Did she know the truth? Allan said he doubted it but he felt one of us should warn her in the morning.

'Drug-takers aren't responsible for their actions,' he said, 'and she has a right to know the possible danger you and she could be in. It's up to her once she knows the facts to forbid Simon the house; inform his stepfather; take what steps she feels are right. I would have told her earlier but I had no proof.'

Poor Simon! I thought again of his childhood and how bitter he was already. Yet for his own sake, he had to try to pull himself together and give up drugs while he still could. For all I knew it might already be too late. If Lady Barclay did forbid him the right to come here, he'd be increasingly bitter and frustrated and thrown even more into the company of the wrong kind of people. Suddenly I remembered the cottage and my new tenants. Instinct had warned me at the time that they were thoroughly unsavoury characters and that I ought not to have agreed to them renting the place. Now I had reason for my antipathy – they, too, might be involved with drugs.

'What's wrong, Jenny?' Allan asked. He must have seen the fear in my face. 'You can trust me, you know. What is it?'

I told him everything, half hoping as I voiced my suspicions that he'd laugh them away, telling me not to be fanciful. But he looked deeply anxious and said flatly:

'You can't go through with it, Jenny. Do you know if the contract is signed?'

I shook my head, I'd let Simon handle everything.

'Well, that'll be the first job I do tomorrow!' Allan said. 'Give me the name and telephone number of your solicitor, Jenny. It's got to be stopped. If necessary, I'll buy the place. I'll raise the money somehow. You say you don't know what Simon's "business" is, or what these men do. They could be drug pushing – anything.'

'Simon said they could supply excellent references to my solicitor,' I argued weakly. How gullible I'd been to believe him.

'Of course they'd have impeccable references!' Allan said. 'But just consider the facts, Jenny. What on earth could two American businessmen want with a cottage like yours, way out in the depth of the country with nothing but charm to commend it. They're businessmen, not tourists wanting to enjoy "a little bit of old England".'

'Supposing contracts have been exchanged?' I said anxiously.

'Well, you've not signed anything, so it should be okay,' Allan reassured me. 'Your solicitor couldn't sign for you and Peter would have to sign too, unless he's given you proxy rights. So don't worry. If you will let me, I'll deal with it for you. Thank God we have found this out in time. Oh, Jenny, I hate the thought of you being here, mixed up in all this. Can't you pack in the job? Go somewhere else?'

I think he knew my answer before I said:

'I couldn't possibly walk out on Lady Barclay even if I wanted to. I'm really deeply attached to her and I'm interested in her book. Besides, she needs someone to look after her.'

'You both need someone to look after you!' Allan said. 'And I'm appointing myself guardian as of now. You're to go to bed, Jenny, and you're not to worry. Leave everything to me, okay?'

I drew a long sigh. Allan had asked for my trust and now that the first moment had come to test it, I had no doubt of any kind that I could trust him – completely. I tried to thank him but he wouldn't even let me begin.

'Bed!' he said firmly and stood up, giving me a feather-light kiss on top of my head. 'I'll look in on Simon and then I'm for bed, too. Goodnight, Jenny. Sleep well – and don't worry.'

I thought I'd never sleep with so much on my mind but almost the same moment as my head touched the pillow I drifted into a deep, dreamless sleep. I was far too tired

173

even momentarily to contemplate why Allan should think he wanted to marry me after the way I'd treated him or to wonder if he had seriously meant what he had said.

10

I lay on a tartan rug on the lawn in the shade of the vast copper beech tree. Bramble panting in an exhausted heap at my feet and old Lady Barclay dozing in a deck chair beside me.

It was the first opportunity I had had for a week to bring my diary up to date. So much seemed to have happened in the past seven days that I was having difficulty recording the events in their correct order.

I chewed the end of my biro and re-read the entry for last Sunday.

'May 16th. Lord Barclay arrived at lunch time and after a private talk with Lady B drove Simon back to London. Lord B not a bit as I expected – nice old boy with silver hair and a gentle smile. He was nice enough to thank me for taking care of his sister and seemed greatly

taken with Allan. Didn't see Simon but Allan said there was a terrible row between him and his step-father. Poor Simon – seems he really is "the black sheep" – Lady B told us some awful things after supper.'

The curtness was perhaps just as well, I thought. I would not have wanted to put in writing some of the wretched stories Lady B told Allan and me about Simon – his conviction at the age of only seventeen in America of drunken driving and Lord Barclay's desperate and unsuccessful efforts to keep him from a prison term in California; his inability on his return to England to hold down any job his step-father found for him; his gambling debts and a dishonoured cheque; his wild extravagance and unpaid bills which Julia had tried to conceal. It was a history of degeneracy that somehow made the fact of his taking drugs seem only to be expected.

Lady Barclay had been at a loss to explain why a boy like Simon, with all his opportunities, should have gone 'bad'. Maybe the death of his own father at an impressionable age had started the rot and Julia's incessant spoiling of the boy had been partly responsible. He had certainly grown up with a grudge against society and there seemed little hope that he would improve.

'Perhaps my brother should have taken a firmer line with Simon,' Lady Barclay said sighing. 'But he always felt a little guilty about Simon – sorry for the boy. And Simon could be very charming when he wished. It was easy to be convinced he meant it when he swore after each escapade to turn over a new leaf and make us all proud of him. I'm sorry for Julia. She's known for years that the boy was no good but hasn't been able to bring herself to face up to it. This time she will have to – my brother will see to that.'

She had turned to me then with a sad little smile.

'Julia obviously felt you were exerting a good influence on Simon, Jenny. She begged me with a humbleness that must have been hard for her seeing how she had always disliked me, not to discourage you from seeing Simon. I was torn between the desire to warn you off him and see if perhaps Simon might be able to reform if he was genuinely fond of you. I should have known better.'

'Wasn't it a little like throwing a lamb to the wolf?' Allan had asked with a hint of reproach in his voice.

My kind old lady had shaken her head.

'Innocence has its own particular protection,' she had said to Allan. 'And my Jenny is much more level headed than you might suppose, Allan. She might have been attracted to Simon but she'd never have fallen in love with him.'

I'd tried to argue that no one but myself could know who I'd fall in love with but Lady B hadn't been convinced. She let me talk myself out and then stubbornly repeated:

'But you'd never have loved him, Jenny dear – not a man you couldn't respect!'

I turned the page of my diary and indeed, felt at that moment as if I were closing a page of my life. Simon would certainly never be a part of it now.

'May 17th. Cabled Peter re cottage at Allan's suggestion, as estate agent has a buyer. Will agree to sell if Peter does. Allan has dealt with the renting to the Americans situation and the contract has been torn up. Allan explained I'll be responsible for expenses so far incurred but reckon it's worth it. Took Bramble for a walk with Allan. Vicar telephoned to say he has news about Edwin Howe. Funny if A turned out to be a Barclay after all. Lady B very excited but Allan quite calm.'

May 18th and 19th had been days given almost entirely to work on *The Crimson Tapestry*. On the 18th I'd discovered irrefutable proof of the existence of Clarissa Barclay in an old letter to the then Lord of the Manor. For the most part this letter dealt with the affairs of the estate, being more an accounting of the head bailiff than of a personal nature. We'd filed it away in a box with other information about the size, state and affluence of the various farms owned by the Barclays of the period and the postscript had been overlooked. It announced the birth of the bailiff's first child, a daughter, and since the birth date coincided so nearly with that of Lord Barclay's newest offspring, requested permission that he and his wife might also name their child Clarissa. Whether permission was granted and the aristocratic and more humbly born children shared the same name we'd never know but the postscript did quite clearly establish the birth of a daughter, Clarissa Barclay. Had his child lived, she would have been seventeen at the time of her elopement with Edwin Howe.

I made no mention of it in my diary but my curiosity was deeply aroused by the

contradictory manner Allan portrayed as more facts were coming to light to prove his relationship with the Barclays. Far from rejoicing about it, he seemed oddly disturbed. I did once ask him why he wasn't showing the same excitement Lady B. and I had been showing but he evaded a real explanation and merely mumbled something vague about his roots being firmly planted in America.

On May 20th I had two telephone calls which upset me – one from Julia begging me not to cut Simon out of my life because of one mishap as she termed it; telling me again and again that he needed me and if I stopped being his friend he might go completely to pieces. The way she put it, I began to feel guilty and in some way responsible for what had happened to Simon, yet logically I knew I had no responsibility in the matter. I'd made no promises of any kind to Simon and we were such comparatively new friends that I didn't see I had any loyalties there, either. I tried to explain there was and never had been anything of any importance between us but she kept reiterating that Simon was madly in love with me, needed me and that I must not desert him.

Her call was followed closely by an even

more embarrassing one from Simon. He simply assumed that I still liked him, was still willing to go out with him and that only the distance between Barclay Manor and London was keeping us apart.

'I can't come down to see you, luv, now they've barred me entry to the stately home, so you'll have to come up to town to see me.'

I began by being as gentle as I could – excusing my inability to get to London on account of my work. But I ended by telling him in plain words that I just did not want to see him again and even that did not have the desired effect. He laughed and said:

'Now don't tell me they've succeeded in frightening you off, my sweet. You've got more guts than that. Just stand up to the lot of them and tell them straight: "I like him and I'm going to go on seeing him!"'

'Simon, I'm not frightened of Them, as you put it, or of you or of myself. I just don't want to see you any more. There's no point. We've nothing in common.'

But he refused to be rebuffed. He told me I'd feel differently in a day or two; that he'd phone again; that he'd never give up; he wanted me and meant to have me. He finally brought Allan's name into it.

'And keep away from the creep, Allan. He wants you, too, and he's got all the advantages down there alone with you, buttering up the Old Trout and making himself out a Knight in Shining Armour. Take my word for it, Jennifer luv, he'd bore you in two minutes flat. You'd never be bored with me, admit it. I've never bored you yet, have I?'

I finally put the phone down. I felt like weeping and yet I wasn't quite sure. Pity for Simon? I didn't know.

And now, today, I simply didn't care. Last night I had had some stupefying news – news that had sent me into a near hysterical mixture of happiness and fear. Peter was coming home. His cable had been brief and factual. *'Do not sell. Flying home 25th. Will 'phone London airport.'*

I was still in a state of semi-shock, my emotions jumping from the wildest hopes that Peter's new romance had gone wrong and he had decided he wanted me after all; and cold logical reasoning that things did not happen in real life the way they did in romantic novels. If Peter was coming home, there would be business or other such mundane reasons why. If he had only told me he loved me. Even one word of endearment such as the word 'Love' before his signature!

181

But there was nothing to guide me and I'd have to wait in suspended activity until the twenty-fifth. Four more days. I didn't know how I could bear it.

I had not yet told either Allan or Lady Barclay my news. I realised that my dear old friend would want to talk about the situation; would probably see the situation through her rose coloured spectacles and tell me that of course Peter loved me; had come home to claim me; that she'd known all along this would happen. I was afraid with her hope and enthusiasm she would raise mine beyond the point where I could control myself if those hopes were dashed.

As for Allan, I realised that the news would not be very welcome. Although he'd never mentioned the words love or marriage again since that night when we'd found Simon drugged, he'd been unable to hide his feelings entirely and I suppose, to be fair, I hadn't discouraged him. I liked him very much; more with each day that passed. In fact, since that night my animosity towards him had vanished and our friendship had taken the most amazing steps forward. We found a hundred and one little things to laugh about; things we had in common and had not realised existed in the other, such as my interest in ornithology. During our walks I'd been able to identify most of the birds we saw and Allan had been as thrilled as I when he heard his very first nightingale singing its heart out late one evening. As a botanist, it was natural that Allan should be interested in Nature and we discovered we each had a secret ambition to go on a real safari in Africa. We found we were both avid readers, loved history, enjoyed the lighter classics of music such as Chopin and Puccini but couldn't get along with Bach or Wagner. We'd neither of us ever skied but both enjoyed skating. In fact, it had almost become a game enumerating everything we had in common. Simon's cautionary remark that I would soon become bored with Allan, had been totally disproved. The more I knew about him the less bored I was. But all these things I liked about Allan were in the mind, so to speak. Physically I was not attracted to him in the way I had been to Simon. I didn't object when Allan held my hand, which he did sometimes on walks, or kissed me good-night lightly on the lips, or put his arm round my shoulders as he sometimes did going into a room. I was aware of him but happy to leave it just there – a casual unimportant intimacy. I certainly didn't think in terms of falling in love with Allan and it came, therefore, as a double surprise when Lady Barclay reacted as she did to my news about Peter.

'There now!' she said in a voice full of chagrin. 'Isn't that just like Fate to put a spoke in the wheel, and everything going so nicely, too!'

Under pressure from me, she admitted she hoped Allan and I were falling in love and she saw Peter's homecoming as one that could only bring me unhappiness.

'If he'd really loved you the way he should, dear, he'd never have left you in the first place,' she said with dismaying logic.

I reminded her that for all she or I knew, Peter was not coming home to 'put the spokes in anyone's wheel' – that she was jumping to conclusions I certainly hadn't accepted and I told her very firmly to stop worrying as I really didn't much care any more whether he came home or not.

If the lie deceived her, I couldn't judge. Her wrinkled old face was enigmatic and inscrutable and for a moment, I had the crazy idea that she was just an old witch, weaving spells to suit herself. Maybe she wished Allan into our lives so she could have the heir she wanted for the Barclays and a satisfactory finale to her book! Maybe she wished Simon on to drugs that night so she could get him out of my life and leave the field free for Allan. Maybe even now she was devising some love portion to make me fall in love with him. Well, her magic could not be very potent. Though I might lie unmoving as a statue on the tartan rug beneath the beech tree, my heart was pounding with tremendous anticipation and my heart was strung so tight with hope that I could only just keep myself in control. Peter still loved me. Peter was coming home for me. Peter wanted me after all ... the phrases rang like repeated bird song in my ears. I had no pride – nor, to myself, did I pretend any. I would, of course, leave Peter to make the running when we met. I wouldn't let him know I still cared unless he did first. But I knew this was only for appearances' sake and that if I could act as I wished, I would rush to London airport to meet his plane and fling myself into his arms and hold him, even if a thousand people looked on with disapproval!

As it was I didn't even know what time his plane arrived and I had to wait for his telephone call; wait for him to offer me Heaven or cast me back into the Hell I'd lived in ever since he went away.

'Oh, well!' Lady Barclay said beside me. 'The good Lord either intends me to finish my book or He doesn't and I must defer to His will as the Bible tells me if your Peter rushes you off to marry you and I have to look for someone else to help me.'

I sat up and put my arms round her knees, hugging her in a sudden rush of remorse and affection. There didn't exist a more saintly woman than my employer and I'd been imagining her as a witch! She'd been so good to me and selfishly, I'd only thought of myself when I knew Peter was coming home. Naturally, she'd been afraid Peter would take me away and she wouldn't be able to finish her book without me.

'You know I'd stay with you just as long as I possibly could, whatever happens,' I said softly. 'I'd like to promise to stay till it is finished regardless of what happens but I can't do that – I still love Peter. If he wanted me to go away with him…'

'My dear, I do understand,' she said. 'It is right that love should come first. My book is the past. What happens to you is the future and that must always come first. Do you know, Jenny, I want your happiness even more than I want to see *The Crimson Tapestry* finished. That's how fond of you

186

I've become. Silly old fool, aren't I!'

I brushed the tears quickly away from my eyes and kissed her. For a moment she looked as if she, too, might cry and then she smiled and said:

'That reminds me of a poem – by a man called Hunt, I think. It couldn't be more appropriate. It goes like this:

'Jenny kiss'd me when we met,
Jumping from the chair she sat in;
Time, you thief, who love to get
Sweets into your list, put that in!
Say I'm weary, say I'm sad,
Say that health and wealth have miss'd me,
Say I'm growing old, but add,
Jenny kiss'd me.'

We were both feeling so emotional I don't think either of us could have said a word. But from behind us Allan, who had appeared from nowhere, said softly:

'I sure would be grateful if you would have Jenny type out the words for me Lady Barclay. It is a charming poem and one I'd like to memorise.'

I suppose it was inevitable that Lady B would mention the fact that Peter was coming home to Allan. In a way I was glad when she did so, relieving me of the task. Somehow I had been putting off doing so though I had not worked out the reason for my reluctance. I must have known subconsciously that Allan's reaction would be far from enthusiastic, although he did what he could to disguise his real feelings with an over cheerful:

'Say, that's wonderful news for you, Jenny. When does he arrive? Will I have the pleasure of meeting him?'

I hastened to point out that I had no idea what Peter's plans were or even the reason for his return to England.

'Maybe he's got the sack!' I said with a flippancy not natural to me. 'Anyway, we'll know soon enough.'

I hoped I sounded casual and disinterested. I could not have borne it if either Allan or dear old Lady B had guessed how desperately I was hoping Peter had had a change of heart. If mine was to be broken a second time, at least no one but I would know it!

'Well, how about giving Bramble a walk now it's a bit cooler,' Allan suggested, changing the subject. 'Okay, Jenny?'

And to my intense relief, the subject of Peter was not raised again.

11

The days, hours, minutes crawled past. I tried to concentrate on my work but I made so many mistakes even my patient employer was forced to chide me.

'I suppose you are on tenterhooks waiting for that boy of yours to telephone!' she said shrewdly, the morning of the day Peter was due home. 'And don't look surprised, Jenny, I hadn't forgotten the date, you know.'

I'm not sure how I managed to live through those next few hours waiting for the 'phone to ring. When it did I was trembling so violently I could hardly hold the receiver. I was afraid to lift it in case when I heard Peter's voice again, he would sound cool, matter of fact, businesslike – anything but the lover.

I need not have tortured myself. Peter's first words were:

'Jenny? Oh, darling, if you only knew how I've longed to hear your voice. Are you there, darling? It's me, Peter!'

I was half laughing, half crying as I hugged

the receiver against my ear. He loved me! He loved me! He loved me!

We talked a lot of nonsense – about how silly we'd been to quarrel, to break our engagement; how we missed each other and so on, and then Peter said:

'I want to see you as soon as possible, darling. Can you meet me in London? Or could I come and see you? Anything you say, sweetheart!'

It was a new, urgent, possessive Peter – the kind of man I'd so longed for him to be. I was overwhelmed.

'Come here!' I told him. 'I'm sure Lady Barclay will make you welcome. Oh, Peter, how long will you be? Will you get a train? It'll be an awful cross country journey.'

'I'll hire a car,' Peter said without hesitation. 'Blow the cost. I've just got to see you as soon as possible.'

I almost did not dare to believe in it. Peter, my careful, money-conscious Peter hiring a car so he could get to me a few hours earlier! Now that this had really happened, I could be glad of our separation if that was what had changed him. All the weeks of misery were more than worth it. I was so happy I tore upstairs to tell Lady Barclay my news.

'Then I'm very happy for you, dear!' she said warmly. 'And of course the young man is more than welcome here. I'll be very interested to meet him. Go and prepare the spare room for him, Jenny. He'll stay the night, of course! And tell Cook there'll be an extra one for dinner tonight and to prepare something special.'

I tore downstairs still wild with excitement and nearly sent poor Allan flying backwards as he came through the front door into the hall. Knowing how fond of me Allan was, it was no doubt cruel of me to gabble out my news but I just couldn't help myself. I wanted everyone to know – to share my happiness. I was only barely conscious of the look that fled in and out of Allan's eyes – miserable and uncertain; then he smiled and said warmly:

'What wonderful news, Jenny. I'll be looking forward to meeting this guy who means so much to you.'

'You'll like him – I know you will!' I cried. 'Oh, Allan, I do want you two to get on well. Peter would be crazy not to like you, too, and I'm sure he will. I hope you'll be great friends. I couldn't bear it if you didn't like each other because I want us to stay friends for always – you and me.'

'I want that too!' Allan said quietly.

As I busied myself preparing the spare room for Peter, I realised that he knew nothing about Allan. There was so much I'd have to tell him ... about Simon and Lady Barclay's book and the awful tenants I'd nearly let our cottage to. The cottage! Now there'd be no need to rent or sell it. Peter and I would live in it after all. It was a fairy tale come true.

I was so emotionally worked up, I suppose it was only natural that my actual meeting with Peter should be a bit of an anti-climax. When I heard the car in the drive and rushed out to meet him, I'd expected the same Peter I'd waved goodbye to at the airport. The man who stepped out of the rented Austin looked quite different. For one thing he'd grown a moustache; for another he was so darkly tanned that he looked more Italian or Spanish than English. But the smile was the same and he held out his arms and I walked slowly into them.

'Oh, Jenny, darling. How pretty you are! I'd almost forgotten!'

He was about to kiss me when Allan came up the drive with Bramble at his heels and Bramble, tearing over to me with his usual extravagant welcome, jumped up between

Peter and me and I had to step back to avoid being scratched on my bare legs. By the time I'd quietened Bramble, Allan was standing waiting to be introduced and our reunion became a more formal social occasion.

'Lady Barclay sent me to tell you she has asked for tea to be served on the lawn by the beech tree,' Allan told me. 'As soon as you've shown Peter his room, would you join her.'

Allan and I helped Peter upstairs with his luggage. The amount he had stowed in the back of the car made me certain Peter had come back to England for good. I was intensely curious to know what had happened but it was another ten minutes before we were alone together. Peter barely waited for Allan to go out through the spare room door before he took me in his arms and began to kiss me with a passionate ardour that I've never known in him before. It took me unawares and made me uneasy – as if I were with a stranger. Peter must have sensed my lack of response for he held me at arms length, breathing deeply as he looked down at me and said:

'What's the matter, Jenny? Don't you love me any more? Didn't you mean what you said on the phone? You're not in love with that American fellow, are you?'

'Of course I still love you,' I said, drawing myself gently away and turning to fiddle with one of the locks on his suitcase. 'And of course I'm not in love with Allan. It's just ... well, you've got to give me a little time to – to adjust. You were the one who was supposed to have stopped loving me, remember. What happened to the girl? My successor!'

Peter covered the few feet between us and tried to put his arms around me again but I shook my head.

'Please tell me what happened. I ... I'm feeling a bit disorientated. I'll be all right as soon as you fill me in with the background.'

Peter sighed, drew out his cigarette case – a crocodile one I'd given him several Christmases ago – and lit a cigarette.

'It was all a dreadful mistake!' he said. 'I should never have taken the job. I loathed every moment of it – no wonder the pay was so good! It needed to be to tempt anyone to work in those conditions. Anyway, I got more and more fed up, bored, lonely, and then Christine came out to visit her father – he was the chap in charge. I'd been missing you dreadfully and well, there she was, pretty, feminine – the first girl I'd seen since I'd waved you goodbye. I thought I was in love. We ... we had an affair and I found out what she was really like – selfish, shallow, a social butterfly type. You know the kind, Jenny. She only slept with me because she was so bored. When she told me she was flying back to England, I suddenly realised how frantically badly I wanted to come home, too. The money just didn't compensate for the boredom and the loneliness. Your cable about the cottage arrived and that was the last straw – I just had to come home – to you, darling.'

I wasn't sure why, but his story failed to ring quite true. Or at least, he was leaving out the bits that mattered. I knew he'd slept with this girl, Christine (and tried not to feel hurt about it) but he hadn't said if he'd fallen in love with her. Since she was the only girl out there, I had to assume that he had loved her for a while anyway, since he'd broken our engagement on her account. And then, his decision to come home – was it because of the dislike of the job or because of me? The way he'd put it, it sounded like the former!

'Darling, you've no need to be the tiniest bit jealous of Christine, I swear it. Our affair didn't mean a thing. I never really stopped loving you, you know. Jenny, what's wrong?'

I didn't know what was wrong. I only

knew that I felt deflated – the intense, nearly delirious happiness of an hour ago dwindled away to feelings of doubt and insecurity; to mistrust of Peter's words, his love, his motives. Perhaps Christine had got bored with him and he had rebounded to me. That wasn't very flattering even if I could overlook what he called his affair. I didn't condemn him on moral grounds – after all, he was a healthy young man and a long way from home. But I couldn't see how, if he'd always loved me, he could have wanted to have a steady affair with another woman. An occasional act of unfaithfulness if he'd been tempted was one thing; a regular arrangement was another.

'We'd better go down to tea,' I said. 'Lady Barclay will be wondering where we are.'

'Who cares!' Peter said, trying once more to take me in is arms, but this time I said bluntly that I did not feel like being kissed right then. He might not care how he behaved towards his hostess but I minded for myself as well as for him how my guest behaved.

Peter looked sulky as we went downstairs and out into the garden. I knew it was my fault we weren't in a better mood but there didn't seem to be anything I could do about it. I still loved him – of course I did – but I didn't want him to take complete possession of me yet; and that was what he seemed to want to do. I couldn't help wondering if it had been his affair with Christine which was making him a much more physical person than the Peter I had known. I knew that I ought to be excited by it but I wasn't – I was only vaguely uneasy and afraid. I was also acutely conscious of Allan's quizzical gaze. It annoyed me even though I realised it was only natural he'd be more than mildly interested in the relationship between Peter and myself. The background to our 'romance' had been somewhat strange to say the least of it and now here was Peter back in my life once more in the most unexpected way. I felt impelled to pay more attention to Peter than I really wished, just to show Allan that all was well again between Peter and myself.

Fortunately Peter was at his best – charming to Lady Barclay, full of little attentions and endearments to me and friendly enough towards Allan. He talked at length about his job and conditions abroad in an interesting way – though he naturally made no mention of Christine! About the future he seemed a bit vague. He intended to rejoin the London branch of the firm who were prepared to keep him on despite the broken contract and hoped that time and hard work would dispel the bad odour which would obviously surround him for a while and put his promotion prospects in jeopardy.

'However, I've learned one thing,' he told Lady Barclay, but glancing at me meaningfully as he did so, 'and that is that money isn't everything. I mean to marry Jenny as soon as possible and make up for the time we've wasted.'

He took hold of my hand and smiled at me affectionately. I ought to have felt elated but all I could feel was resentful. He'd shot off abroad and left me, broken our engagement, had an affair with another girl and now was talking as if nothing had ever happened to mar our relationship; as if he took it quite for granted that I would be waiting with total forgiveness to rush up the aisle to the altar the moment he suggested it.

As unobtrusively as possible, I withdrew my hand, pretending to fondle Bramble's long silky ears as if my mind were elsewhere. As casually as I could I said:

'Of course we can't get married for a little while, Lady Barclay. I mean, I wouldn't dream of leaving here until *The Crimson Tapestry* is finished.'

My dear old lady looked at me from beneath her spectacles.

'Jenny, you know you're quite free to leave any time you wish,' she said. 'I'm not saying I could replace you, but if you and Peter are going to live in the cottage – why, you could continue coming here to help me during the day, couldn't you?'

I felt cornered.

'We'll see!' I said vaguely. 'Peter and I haven't really had time yet to discuss things.'

'Of course not!' Lady Barclay said apologetically. 'I'm getting so old and stupid I never thought. Now you two run along and leave Allan and me to finish the cucumber sandwiches on our own. I know they play havoc with my digestion but I'm old enough now to indulge myself even if it is unwise.'

I would have been quite happy staying where I was but Peter was already on his feet holding out his hand and I couldn't think of an excuse for staying. Lady Barclay had Allan for company and, I told myself firmly, it was high time I faced up to my problems and stopped running away from them.

I took Peter down to the old summer

house. It was disused now and inside it was dusty and cobwebby and full of spiders and other insects. But outside, on the tiny veranda there was a wrought iron seat and a beautiful view of the house from across the lawns. I could just make out the dark shadow that was Allan stretched out on the grass beneath the beech tree, his head propped up on his arm and the shadowy form of Lady Barclay, her face inclined towards them. They were obviously deep in conversation and I could not help but wonder if they were discussing Peter and me.

'Jenny, darling!' Peter reached for my hand and held it tight between both of his, his voice sounding reproachful so that I knew he was aware that my thoughts had not been with him. I was still evading the issue, I thought. With an effort I turned to look directly at him.

'Yes, Peter, I'm listening.'

'Darling, you sounded very uncertain about wanting to get married right away. Perhaps I should have said something to you first. You aren't angry with me, are you?'

'Angry? Of course not!' My voice sounded far from reassuring even to me!

'Upset, then? Darling, do tell me what's going on in that mind of yours. You *do* still love me, don't you? You said on the 'phone that you did; that you'd never stopped caring and were so pleased I'd come home.'

I nodded, unable to deny that impulsive outburst.

'Then why the prevarication now? You do still want to marry me, don't you?'

'Yes, of course. It's just a matter of time, Peter. After all, a week ago I thought you were going to marry someone else – Christine!'

Peter's face darkened.

'But that's absurd. Of course I'd never marry a girl like that. I only broke off our engagement because I felt it wasn't fair to you to keep you tied whilst I…'

'Were having an affair with another girl?'

I could not prevent my words sounding bitter.

Peter was instantly contrite.

'Try not to blame me too much, Jenny. You were miles away and I was lonely.'

'I was lonely too!' I said. But my words brought back the memory of Simon and how very nearly I had been tempted to be unfaithful to Peter. Who was I to blame when in fact I'd let two men kiss me if I counted Allan as one, and had in my heart wanted Simon to make love to me. I shuddered at the thought. Now that I knew what Simon was really like beneath the fascinating exterior, I was appalled at how nearly I had succumbed. If Peter knew! But I had no intention of telling him. Some nasty, vindictive part of my nature wanted to make him suffer the way I had suffered because of him.

We spent an hour discussing the past. Peter was more contrite every minute. He accepted all the blame and asked only that we could forget the whole miserable interlude and go back to the happier state of our engaged days. I shook my head.

'I think we were engaged far too long, Peter,' I said. 'That was part of the trouble.'

His face lighted up.

'There, Jenny, you are agreeing with me. We should get married at once. You haven't let the cottage go, have you? We've got a home all ready for us. There's nothing whatever to stop us marrying next week if we want.'

I suppose not. In a way, I wanted to be able to say yes. At the same time I wanted to make Peter wait. Perhaps it was pride and I wished to show him I wasn't going to be picked up and put down at his whim.

'Just give me a few days to get used to you

being home,' I said at last. 'Then we'll set a date.'

He put his arms round me then and kissed me. I felt quite numb. For days and nights I'd longed to be back in Peter's arms and to feel, as I could now, that he really loved me and wanted me. Now that the moment had come, I did not seem able to feel anything at all. It was unnerving – the more so in that Peter at once noticed my lack of response and said in a small hurt voice:

'You've changed, Jenny. I don't know what it is about you but you're different.'

'You've changed, too!' I countered. But then I knew what had changed him – Christine.

Peter looked suddenly happier.

'I suppose I have,' he agreed. 'Well, maybe you're right, darling, and we need a week or two to get to know one another again. Let's start right away, Jenny. I want to know everything that's been happening.'

So I filled him in – elaborating and exaggerating a bit, I suppose, so that he wouldn't think I'd been sitting around twiddling my thumbs. I told him nearly everything there was to tell about Simon, admitting I had found him attractive. Allan's name cropped up occasionally, of course, but Peter only showed interest when I told him Allan had once said he wanted to marry me.

'Seriously?' he asked, as if surprised.

'Well, of course he was serious!' I hit back hurt. 'Why shouldn't he? You do!'

Privately I had reached the conclusion that Allan had not been in the least serious, or if he had been, it had sprung from a momentary emotion. Since we'd had our talk, our relationship had settled into a comfortable platonic affection which I had found easy and satisfying. If Allan had really fallen in love with me, he would hardly have felt able to accept me merely as a friend! But I wasn't going to admit this to Peter. I wanted him to be jealous – the way I was jealous of Christine.

'Now tell me about her,' I said. 'I've told you all there is to tell about me.'

But Peter seemed reluctant to say much. He admitted she was very attractive, petite, dark, vivacious – my opposite, in fact. She was twenty-two, rich, spoilt and very sophisticated. I had the impression that Peter had been a great deal more fascinated by her than Christine had been attracted to him. All the same, she must have loved him to have been willing to have an affair with him.

'Don't let's talk about her!' Peter said when I tried to question him further. 'I'm not likely to see her again, ever, and I'd rather forget her. You have to believe me when I tell you that it was just an interlude I'm ashamed of and don't want to think about or talk about. I'd be happy if you'd forget it, too, darling.'

But I didn't think it would be all that easy for me. If Peter could be unfaithful to me once, it could happen again. How could I be sure? I wanted to trust him but the trust was not there. Maybe it would return in time. I needed time. I wanted very badly to feel close to him again. In an effort to achieve this, I suggested we walked down to our cottage and looked over the home that had once meant so much to us both. Surely there, I thought, if nowhere else, we would be able to regain that faith in our future.

I let him take hold of my hand and together we set off down the drive towards the little house that was one day to be my home.

12

We never reached the cottage. We were crossing the drive when I heard Allan shouting my name and his tone of voice left me in no doubt that something terrible had happened. I forgot Peter and ran to meet Allan.

'Jenny, it's Lady Barclay. She's had some kind of collapse!' Allan gasped breathlessly, his face drawn with anxiety. 'You go and stay with her while I telephone for the doctor. Quick as you can!'

My heart thumping, I raced back across the lawn. I could see Lady Barclay, a diminutive figure, lying back in the garden chair, Allan's jacket laid over her. The sunlight was still filtering through the heavily leafed branches of the beech tree, casting dappled patches of golden light over the quiet, peaceful scene. A thrush was singing furiously on one of the boughs and a wasp buzzed noisily in one of the empty teacups. It just did not seem possible that anything could be wrong in such a calm, idyllic setting. Yet as soon as I drew near I could see the dreadful grey white pallor of Lady Barclay's face and fear struck coldly at me.

I sank to my knees beside her chair and took one frail blue veined hand between my own.

'It's me, Jenny! I'm here. I'll look after you!' I babbled incoherently. The old lady's eyes were closed and I did not think she understood what I was saying but her eyelids flickered and she murmured:

'Such a pain, Jenny. Such a pain!'

My mind raced with horrible possibilities, a heart attack being the most fearful. I felt so helpless and terrified that she would die before the doctor could get here.

'Is it serious, do you think?' Peter asked beside me.

I had forgotten him. I put my finger to my lips warning him that Lady Barclay might hear him. I wished desperately that Allan would return and reassure me. I had always known how fond I'd become of Lady Barclay but now that I was afraid she was going to die, I realised that I loved her; that she was as dear to me as the grandmother I'd never known.

After what seemed an hour but was only ten minutes, Allan returned carrying a tartan rug.

'The doctor's on his way,' he told me. 'He said not to move her but to keep her warm.'

Gently, he tucked the rug round the tiny body, and kneeling on the opposite side of the chair, took Lady Barclay's other hand, holding it as I was doing.

'Don't worry!' he whispered. 'The doctor will be here soon.'

Lady Barclay seemed suddenly to become worse. Her body twisted and she moaned in pain and complained of feeling very sick. I thought the doctor would never come but at last he did so and within a few minutes, dispelled any ideas were might have had about a heart attack.

'I've little doubt it is some form of food poisoning,' he said. 'Her heart is perfectly all right, considering the strain that the present pain is having on her. We must get her back to the house at once.'

Allan carried her in his arms as easily as he would have carried a child. I ran ahead to prepare her bed and collect the items the doctor told me he would want. Peter was despatched to telephone the hospital with further requests. The hospital was twenty miles away and too far, Dr Farran thought, to take the patient.

Within an hour Lady Barclay's room had

become the scene of intense and efficient activity. Dr Farran's assistant and a private nurse were fighting to keep up the old lady's strength whilst they rid her body of the poison that had caused the attack. Downstairs, Allan and I sat drinking coffee and waiting with taut strained nerves to hear if she would survive. Peter had gone to his room feeling that he would only be in the way and could be most helpful by removing himself.

Allan had telephoned Lord Barclay and he was on his way down from London. We had discussed the necessity for ringing Julia but had decided to leave this decision with Lady Barclay's brother when he arrived. There was nothing more either of us could do but wait.

There was no doubt now that my poor old lady was suffering from some form of poisoning. I could not leave the subject alone.

'I simply don't understand it!' I said to Allan for the twentieth time. 'We all eat the same meals. Surely if she had had something that was off, we'd have been affected, too.'

We were still going through the menus of the last two days when Dr Farran came into the room. He looked tired but jubilant.

'I think she's going to be all right,' he told us. 'It's a miracle, really, seeing her age. We had to use a stomach pump of course. My assistant is taking a sample straight to the laboratory for analysis and we'll soon know what caused the trouble. She'll need very careful nursing and I've arranged for Nurse Meadows to stay here for the next week anyway. Is that going to cause domestic difficulties?'

I assured him that it would not. Once again we went over the food we'd all eaten but the problem remained insoluble and was put aside until the results of the analysis came through.

'The main thing now is to try to get her strength back,' Dr Farran said. 'At her age … well…'

He could not wait for Lord Barclay's arrival, having a busy evening surgery awaiting him, but he promised to speak to him later on the telephone. He would in any case, ring up as soon as the hospital notified him about the analysis.

Allan saw him to the door and I went upstairs to see if there was anything I could do. As I entered Lady Barclay's room I could see that my presence wasn't needed. The dark-haired girl called Nurse Meadows

was sitting in a chair by Lady Barclay's bed, looking calm and reposed and she smiled as I came in.

'My name is Angela Meadows,' she said in a friendly way. 'We didn't have time to introduce ourselves downstairs.'

I smiled back, liking her instantly. She was a bit older than I and pretty, with jet-black hair and green eyes. I was sure from the faint brogue in her voice and from her looks that she was Irish.

I introduced myself, told her about Allan and Peter and that Lord Barclay was due to arrive at any moment. Lady Barclay was sleeping so we talked in whispers. Angela, though she looked professional enough in her neat blue and white uniform, and clearly knew her job, was nevertheless young enough not to stand on any formality. We agreed to use Christian names and then Angela asked me about Allan and Peter. She wanted to know which one was my boy friend.

'They're both frightfully attractive!' she said with a charmingly impish grin. 'So I'd better know the score right from the start!'

I suppose my silence must have made her think she had overstepped the mark somehow. It was certainly not my intention to put

her in her place. After all, I was an employee here just as she was and our positions were equal. There was no reason why she should not approach me as one girl to another and my hesitation was not from any desire to be unfriendly. I began a stammering explanation before she could complete the apology she had begun to make. It was simply that I hadn't been able to think of the right description for Peter, I told her. We had been engaged and were affianced, but then we'd broken off the engagement. Now Peter had come home and we were intending to get married but we weren't re-engaged.

Angela smiled, relaxing.

'That's all right then!' she said. 'I was afraid I'd overstepped the mark asking personal questions like that when we'd only just met. It's my impulsive Irish temperament, I'm afraid. My mother is forever telling me it'll get me into trouble and sure enough it does. In my profession one should think first and speak after!'

We talked for a minute or two about Lady Barclay. Angela seemed cheerfully optimistic about her recovery.

'It's surprising how tough some of these tiny little old ladies can be,' she said. 'It's the hefty ones that go quickest. You're very fond

of her, aren't you?'

'We both are,' I said, including Allan. 'I don't think I could bear it if anything happened to her now. She wants so desperately to finish her book.' I explained briefly about *The Crimson Tapestry*. Then about Allan's possible connection with the Barclay family. 'I think she would die quite willingly if she could actually prove he was a relative,' I said. 'She's so immersed in the family history that I don't think she can stand the thought that the family will cease to exist when she and her brother die.'

We discussed Allan's investigations a few minutes longer and then I went off to prepare a room for Angela in Lady Barclay's little sitting room next door. Allan and Peter would have to carry a bed into it and I wanted to clear a space first.

I tidied up the papers on my desk, collecting the half typed chapter I had been working on that morning whilst waiting for Peter to telephone me. It seemed fantastic that it had been only this morning. Time was strange, I thought. It had been such a long and eventful day and I had gone through so many different emotions that it was small wonder I was exhausted.

I picked up Lady Barclay's tapestry from

the armchair where she had left it. It was so nearly finished, the beautiful rich reds and blues merging softly with one another in the intricate heraldic design. It was amazing that with her failing eyesight, the old lady could still see well enough to make those tiny stitches. I put it in her sewing drawer together with the wools. Maybe when she was better she would want to do some work in bed. It would be a tragedy if she were unable to complete it.

I tried to stop myself thinking such thoughts. Death had seemed so close this past hour or two. I had been made to see how vulnerable anyone as old as Lady Barclay was to sudden ending of life. Other people could suffer food poisoning without real danger but at her age...

I kept myself busy, not wishing to dwell on such thoughts. I comforted myself with the hopeful way both Dr Farran and Angela Meadows had spoken. I knew Lady Barclay had faith in the elderly doctor who had attended her for years; and soon Lord Barclay would be here to take full responsibility. Neither Allan nor I were really in a position to ask for second opinions or specialists even if we had wanted to.

Suddenly I remembered Peter and bit my

lip. What kind of home-coming had he had? I asked myself guiltily. Lady Barclay meant nothing to him naturally, and he must be feeling very neglected.

I went to his room and asked him if he would help Allan move a bed into Lady Barclay's sitting-room for the nurse. Peter was sitting in the armchair by the window reading a book. He stood up as I came into the room and was willing enough to help but wanted me to kiss him first.

'I've hardly had you to myself for two consecutive minutes the whole day!' he complained – with reason. 'Come here and kiss me, darling.'

I let him put his arms round me and lifted my face, trying to will myself into the same mood as his. He had not the worries I had had, I excused myself as his lips came down hard on mine and his arms tightened around me. I wanted to get Angela's room finished before Lord Barclay arrived and I'd still to find Allan whom I'd not seen since the doctor left. Then I must make sure the Polish couple realised there would be five for the evening meal which must be laid properly in the dining-room for Lord Barclay. I wasn't quite sure whether Angela and I, as employees, would be expected to dine with him. There was so much to think of and...

'Jenny, what's wrong? If that's the kind of welcome I've come home to, I'll begin to wish I hadn't come home at all.'

'Oh, Peter, I'm sorry!' I said, aware that my mind had been miles away. 'Please try to understand ... I've been so upset!'

His face softened and he drew me back against him.

'I know darling, and I want to make you forget all about it for a moment. Just remember that I love you and you love me and nothing else in the world matters but us.'

'But it does!' I cried involuntarily. 'I love Lady Barclay. If she dies...'

'If she dies we'll be married right away!' said Peter firmly. 'I'll look after you, Jenny. Everything will be the way we always planned.'

I wanted to feel reassured, to really believe as Peter did in our future; to believe in him. Yet I seemed numb – unable to respond as I should; as I had secretly imagined I would when Peter was half a world away. Now I stood held against him, his arms round me, his mouth against mine and I felt nothing – no stirring of my senses, not even satisfaction that Peter should love me the way he appeared to do now; the way I'd always wanted.

I could hear Bramble barking furiously down in the drive; followed closely by the sound of tyres churning up the gravel as the brakes of a car pulled up outside the front door. I detached myself gently from Peter's arms and said:

'That must be Lord Barclay. I'd better go down, Peter. Could you and Allan move one of these beds for me?' I explained quickly what I wanted done. Peter sighed, as if annoyed by the interruption but he followed me out on to the landing and went off in search of Allan.

I ran downstairs and in the library I gave Lord Barclay a summary of the afternoon's events. He looked tired and terribly worried. I did my best to reassure him and he thanked me for everything I had done, nodding his approval of keeping a full time nurse to care for his sister. He seemed to think he should have her moved to the London Clinic but I explained that Dr Farran thought it best she stayed in her own home.

Lord Barclay nodded.

'I suppose he's right. My sister loves this house – when you get old home means a great deal.'

Lady Barclay was still sleeping when he went up to see her. Angela promised him he need have no worries for the time being. Dr Farran expected her condition to remain unchanged but that she was to telephone him if there were any signs at all of a deterioration.

'I am fully qualified to deal with these emergencies,' she said.

'She looks so young to have all those qualifications,' Lord Barclay sighed as we went back downstairs. 'But then all you young people these days are much more efficient than you look. You, my dear, have proved a tremendous help to my sister. She speaks to me of you with such warmth and pleasure. And the young man – the American. I gather he is staying here. I'm looking forward to meeting him. Sybil tells me he could very well be a Barclay – my heir, in fact. I'd like to get to know the fellow. You don't think he is a charlatan, do you?'

I smiled.

'No, I don't, Lord Barclay. Whether he is a Barclay or not, one thing I am sure of and that is that he is a hundred per cent genuine. I think you'll like him. My ... my fiancé is here, too. He arrived before Lady

Barclay became ill and she invited him to stay the night. I hope you don't mind.'

'Indeed not! I'll look forward to meeting him, too. Engaged, are you? Don't rush into marriage, my dear. Never does to be in too great a hurry. Marry in haste, repent at leisure, eh? But then you young ones are always impatient. I suppose I was too, at your age.'

I remembered his words later that evening. Lord Barclay had retired to his study, Angela had returned to the sick room and Peter was making a telephone call to London to arrange with a cousin of his to make room for him at his flat for the next few weeks. I said I'd give Bramble a last stroll round the garden and Allan offered to accompany me.

We walked in silence at first, each of us lost in our own thoughts. Then Allan said suddenly:

'Peter seems a nice guy, Jenny. All the same, don't rush into marriage. I know it's none of my business and I'm really the very last person who should advise you. All the same, promise me you'll take time to think about it.'

I could smell the scent of the azaleas heavy on the soft night air. An owl was hooting somewhere down the drive and the dew was shining with a strange phosphorescence in the moonlight. For some reason my senses were acutely alive to these things. Allan was smoking one of his American cigarettes and the tobacco smell was drifting across to me on the faintest of night breezes. I wished desperately that he had not spoken. Until that moment I had been oddly content. Now all the uneasiness of the day rushed over me and I shivered.

'Have I offended you?'

I shook my head.

'No, of course not. You're a friend and you've a right to say what you think. Free speech and all that,' I added flippantly.

'But not an unbiased friend,' Allan said quietly. 'I'm trying desperately for your sake to be objective but it's only fair to admit I couldn't be completely so.'

'Whyever not?' I asked. 'You've nothing against Peter – or me, I hope?'

'Oh, Jenny!' Allan's voice sounded vaguely despairing – the way it might have done were he addressing a child who would not understand something he was trying to explain in simple terms. He hesitated and then said: 'No, I'm not going to say anything more. I don't want to influence you. You have to make your own decisions.'

I felt let down. It was as if Allan were shelving all responsibility for me. Yet when I stopped to consider it, why should he be responsible in any way at all? As he had said, I had to make my own decisions. If only I knew what I wanted! Did I love Peter? And if I did, why wasn't I as ecstatic with happiness as I surely ought to have been when he held me in his arms and told me he loved me? Would it all come right after a day or two and I would start to feel something positive again? Numbness seemed to have taken complete control of me.

'It's getting cold,' Allan spoke beside me. 'Better go in.' He whistled for Bramble who came obediently out of the undergrowth, wagging his stumpy tail and showering my bare legs with dew. We turned and walked back towards the house. Lady Barclay's room was lit with a faint glow. Allan must have been glancing in that direction, too, for he said:

'What an attractive girl that young nurse is. Seems nice, too.'

'I think so, too,' I agreed. 'I'm glad we haven't a starchy old matron living with us for the next week or so. Angela's Irish.'

'Then that explains her soft lilting voice!'

Allan said. 'And the wicked twinkle in her eye!'

I was surprised somehow, to hear Allan say such things. I remembered that Angela had said she thought Allan attractive and I supposed they'd been flirting – though Allan and flirtations didn't seem to go together. At the same time, he was an unattached young man and Angela an extremely pretty girl – it was perfectly normal that they should be attracted to each other.

'The attraction seems to be mutual then,' I said, telling him of Angela's remark about him and Peter. In the darkness Allan laughed.

'Oh, I don't think I made much impression. It was your Peter who did most of the talking...' He broke off as if regretting his remark. Perhaps he thought I'd be jealous because Peter had been chatting up some other girl. Maybe I should have felt a twinge of jealousy, but I did not. It must be part of the same inertia I'd been feeling all day.

As we went into the house Lord Barclay came to the door of the study and called to us. Whilst we had been out Dr Farran had telephoned with the results of the analysis. His face white and shocked, Lord Barclay informed us that the stomach had contained a small amount of arsenic.

Allan and I stared at him aghast. The old man looked embarrassed.

'You realise, of course, that this is rather serious. My sister certainly would not have taken arsenic knowingly. Someone must have given her something containing the poison. The matter will have to be investigated.'

Allan found his voice first.

'Jenny and I were discussing earlier what Lady Barclay could have eaten to upset her, Sir,' he said. 'As far as we can ascertain she had exactly the same food we ate. It's impossible she could have been given arsenic in her food or we would be ill, too.'

'So I understand from the cook whom I've already questioned,' Lord Barclay said. 'Tomorrow we have to compile a complete list of what was eaten by all of you. I'm sorry – but this is a matter I have now to put in the hands of the police. I have to protect my sister. Someone has tried to harm her and may try again.'

I felt physically sick with shock. Allan took my arm and steadied me. Somehow he guided me out of the study and into the dining-room. I slumped into a chair, shivering.

'But who could want to do such a thing? To Lady Barclay of all people! I don't understand. I don't understand!'

Allan went over to the sideboard and poured out a small measure of brandy. He stood by me insisting I drink it.

'It's been a pretty difficult day for you,' he said. 'Come on, Jenny. You'll feel better if you drink it even if you don't like it.'

It did revive me. I felt suddenly warmer and very angry.

'There has to be a mistake!' I said. 'I just won't believe anyone would want to murder my poor old girl. Why, everyone loves her!'

My mind, working overtime now, sought for possible suspects. I would swear that the Polish couple were incapable of such a thing. They'd been with Lady Barclay since before the war – thirty-two years. They'd come as refugees from Poland and she'd given them a home, a new life. They adored her. There had been only Allan and myself in the house until Peter arrived at teatime. Lady Barclay had not left the house to have a meal elsewhere so who could have given her arsenic?

'There must have been a mistake at the laboratory,' I said again. 'There's no other explanation.'

'I would like to think you are right,' Allan said as much to himself as to me. 'But hospitals don't make mistakes like that. There has to be an explanation. I hear your British police are wonderful. No doubt they will solve this – though heaven knows how!'

Suddenly I remembered Peter. When Allan and I had left the house to take Bramble for a last run, he'd been phoning. Since our return I'd forgotten all about him. The thought brought the colour rushing to my cheeks. No matter what the pressures on me, how could I forget his very existence! What was he doing, I wondered frantically. Had he gone to bed in disgust? Ought I to go up and explain what had delayed me?

'Something wrong?'

I felt the guilty colour rushing to my cheeks again. This was something I could not discuss with Allan. I shook my head and pretended a yawn.

'Just tired,' I lied. 'I'll say goodnight, Allan. It's been a long day and I'm for my bed.'

Allan did not question me further though I had the impression he did not believe my lie. He was tactful enough to say goodnight at once and left the house to go across to his flat.

I went slowly upstairs. As I neared the

225

spare room, I heard voices coming from Lady Barclay's sitting-room. A man's voice and a woman's. Was Lord Barclay visiting his sister again, I wondered. But the question was answered almost at once as the sitting-room door opened and Peter came out on to the landing. He was smiling, but when he saw me his expression changed and he looked – not guilty exactly but embarrassed.

'Oh, there you are!' he said awkwardly. 'I was just having a word with Angela.'

I couldn't think of anything to say. There was no reason at all why Peter should not have looked in to say goodnight to the nurse – maybe even gone there in search of me. Had it not been for his obvious embarrassment, I don't think I would have thought about it.

'I hope you don't mind,' he said, looking and sounding even more ill at ease.

'Of course not!' I said. Why *should* I mind, I thought. Or did Peter imagine I might be jealous?

I felt a sudden hysterical desire to laugh. If Peter knew that a few minutes ago I'd clean forgotten his existence, he would be the one to mind.

We stood in silence, avoiding each other's eyes. I did not seem able to make any kind of move. It seemed unbelievable that there could be this constraint between us. We were more like strangers than two young people who were going to get married and meeting for the first time together after weeks of separation. There must be something wrong with me, I thought ruefully. I did not seem able to behave the way people normally behaved. I suppose that deep down inside me I was still hurt and angry and resentful of the way Peter had left me and an excess of pride was preventing me now from giving him too big a welcome home.

As if he too had been thinking along these lines, Peter suddenly took a step nearer to me and put two hands on my shoulders, saying:

'Jenny, you do still love me?'

The words hung between us. I wanted to say: 'Yes, of course I do,' but the words would not come. I prevaricated.

'What makes you ask that? Don't you still love me?'

'You've changed … somehow…' he said uncertainly. 'You just don't seem particularly glad I'm here. Oh, I don't know what it is but it's hardly the reunion I had been expecting.'

I moved back imperceptibly so that his

hands fell away from my shoulders.

'You seem to forget I had no idea until you telephoned me this morning that you were coming home ... to *me!*'

My voice sounded stiff and unloving. I could not help it.

'Yes, I suppose that is my own fault. I should have included that in my cable when I made up my mind to come home. Only I wasn't sure...'

'How I'd be feeling?' I broke in. 'Or whether you still loved me?'

Peter looked away as if unwilling to meet my eyes.

'A bit of both, really, I suppose,' he admitted. 'After all, quite a bit of water had gone under the bridge for both of us. As a matter of fact, I don't think I realised time hadn't exactly stood still for you either. I mean, well, you'd written and told me about Simon but you didn't tell me about Allan. Just what has been going on between you?'

I felt a moment of pure feminine triumph. Peter was jealous. Now he might understand how I was feeling about his affair with Christine.

'You could say Allan and I were "just good friends",' I said with what I felt was clever ambiguity. Let Peter make what he would of that! But my moment was short lived, for Peter said gloomily:

'I suppose I've no right to object, whatever you've been up to, seeing the way I behaved. All the same, Jenny, if we are going to get married we ought...'

'*If?*' I broke in. 'Then there is a doubt in your mind?'

'Well, if there's a doubt in yours, naturally there is an "if". Maybe we shouldn't rush things, Jenny. Maybe we need a bit of time to ... to get to know each other again. I've felt all day as if I were with ... someone else – not my Jenny at all. Maybe I'm wrong.'

I wanted to tell him that it was hardly the kind of day when anyone could behave normally – what with Lady Barclay's collapse and all the distractions that had accompanied it. But I didn't feel like making excuses. Instead, I asked him if he had planned to go to London tomorrow, explaining that if so, he had better cancel any arrangements he had made.

'Lord Barclay says that the police will be coming to question everyone in the house,' I told him.

Peter looked shaken.

'They can hardly suspect me of wanting to

do the old girl in!' he said. 'What motive could I have had?'

'Or any of us for that matter,' I argued.

'Well, your American boy friend had a motive, didn't he? I thought he had just about proved he was the last surviving Barclay. The sooner the old girl and her brother kick the bucket, the sooner he'd inherit!'

I was too surprised to react instantly, otherwise I might have hit him. By the time I'd recovered I was just angry.

'That's about the most childishly idiotic thing I ever heard anyone say!' I flung at him. 'And if that's the way your mind is running, then I don't want to stay out here talking to you.'

I walked away quickly, ignoring his voice calling to me. At that moment I hated him; hated him out of all proportion to the offence. After all, Peter did not know Allan and could easily be excused for thinking badly of him. What I think I hated him for most of all was for putting the idea in my mind that Allan did have a motive, however unlikely, however unbelievably, however improbable. Alone of us all he was the one who did stand to gain if Lady Barclay died – *if* he were a Barclay. No one in a million years would be able to convince me that

Allan had it in him to be a murderer – I could laugh at the thought. But, I asked myself as I tossed and turned sleeplessly in my bed, would the police?

For the first time since we'd met, I began to hope desperately that Allan's efforts to prove his connection to the Barclay family were meaningless and that facts would show that he had no connection at all.

13

The ensuing day was almost as nightmarish as the one preceding it. The house, usually so quiet and uneventful, was a bustle of people coming and going. First there was the doctor to visit Lady Barclay who, mercifully, was beginning to show signs of recovery. Soon after, the police arrived and we were interviewed in turn in the library. Having given an account of my own position in the household, the officer began to question me about Allan. How long had I known him? What did I know of him? What were his relations with Lady Barclay? With Lord Barclay? With the stepson, Simon?

I refused to do more than vouch for the fact that Allan and Lady Barclay had always been the best of friends; that I knew she trusted him completely and that I personally had no reason to doubt him in any way. Then I suggested somewhat pertly that they ask Allan himself whatever else they wished to know. He would most certainly be able to substantiate his position with the American university and that he was on a six months' Sabbatical. I was asked about Peter, denied that I was still engaged to him and declined to give my reasons. In all, I don't think I made a very good impression but I didn't care. I was far too concerned at Allan's position in all this and wondered if I should suggest to him that he contacted my solicitor and ask him to act for him.

I hung about in the hall until Allan came out of the library. It was a relief to see him looking reasonably cheerful.

'Oh, Allan, I'm so worried!' I said impulsively.

He looked surprised.

'I can't think why! I think I managed to put all their minds at rest.' Seeing my face, he laughed. 'Why, Jenny, *you* didn't think I could have harmed a hair of the old lady's head, did you?'

But I couldn't joke about it.

'Of course not!' I said crossly. 'But others might think you had a motive.'

'Others?' Allan repeated the word questioningly. But he did not pursue the matter. Instead he produced a letter from his jacket pocket and handed it to me. 'This came by the morning post,' he told me. 'It's from the Vicar.'

As I read the neat scholarly handwriting I realised that I was holding the proof that Lady Barclay had been searching for – Allan's connection with the Barclay family. The Vicar, searching through old Parish records, had come across a letter from Percy, Lord Barclay, asking the Vicar of that date to erase the name of his daughter, Clarissa, from the records, *because of the greate shame brought upon our family honour by her untimely elopement with Edwin Howe.* The letter went on to say that the young couple *had set sail for the new World and it is my wish that neither one should be spoken of again and it is to be as if they were dead.*

I stared up at Allan with a mixture of feelings – pleasure because I knew how happy this would make Lady Barclay, but with concern for Allan himself who must surely now come under suspicion. The news did not seem to have made him particularly happy.

'Aren't you pleased?' I asked curiously.

'In a way, I suppose I am. But I belong in America, Jenny. I could never make my permanent home in England. If I really am the last of the Barclays, I imagine it would fall to me to take care of the estate, this house, the family affairs. I'm simply not qualified to do so, even if I wanted to.'

I felt a surge of disappointment. Poor Lady Barclay – to have found an heir who had no wish to inherit! Yet I could understand that Allan had a career of his own he wanted to pursue. It was unreasonable to expect him to want to throw up his past and start life again in this quiet corner of England where he must feel a total stranger.

'Would nothing persuade you to live in England?' I asked. 'A great many Americans would jump at the chance to become Lord of the Manor.'

'Then obviously I am not typical!' Allan said. He gave me a long searching look. 'Maybe in time I might get used to the idea – I don't know. I love England and I love the countryside round here. In a funny kind of way it's got to seem like a second home. But fond as I am of Lady Barclay, I can't imagine myself living here alone with her. I'd need a greater incentive, Jenny, a much greater incentive.'

'Such as?' I prompted him as he paused.

'Such as a wife and children to live here with me.'

'But, Allan, the chances are you will get married long before Lord Barclay dies. Why, he's only just seventy. He could live another ten years or more.'

Allan turned away.

'But I shan't be marrying anybody, Jenny, if I can't marry you,' he said quietly.

I felt the colour burning in my cheeks. Stupidly, I'd allowed the conversation to become personal. Innocently, too, for I'd imagined we had become good friends and nothing more. I'd pushed to the back of my mind that extraordinary evening when Allan had told me he intended to marry me, refusing to take it seriously. Now he had forced me to accept that he'd meant what he had said.

'I'm going to marry Peter!'

'Yes, I know!'

'Then it's just plain silly to talk the way you were, Allan. Besides, you can't really mean any of it. You aren't any more in love with me than I am with you.'

'Or you with Peter!'

We were almost shouting at each other.

'I do love him – I've always loved him,' I said. 'How can you judge what I feel? I just wish you'd go away and mind your own business.'

'As a matter of fact I am going – just as soon as this wretched business over Lady Barclay has been cleared up. I've no wish to stay and see your life in ruins, Jenny – for that's what will happen. You're no more in love with Peter than ... than he is with you!'

My anger boiled over and, deliberately, I stepped forward and slapped Allan's face as hard as I could. The moment I had done so, my temper cooled and I backed away expecting some violent reaction from him. To my total astonishment he was smiling.

'I'm glad you did that, Jenny!' he said softly. 'Now I know you care.'

He turned and walked away from me, leaving me near to tears and completely bewildered. What had he meant? That he now realised I did love Peter? Or that he was crazy enough to think I cared about *him?* And where was Peter? I hadn't seen him since breakfast.

I made my way upstairs to see if Lady Barclay was sufficiently recovered for me to sit with her a little while. I found Angela just coming out of Lady Barclay's bedroom carrying a tray of sick-room paraphernalia. It would be better not to disturb her, she told me, as she was still fairly dopey.

'I'm just going to make a cup of coffee,' she said. 'Would you like one? Peter found me an electric kettle and a jar of Nescafé so we don't need to go down to the kitchen.'

I suppose my mind did register the fact that she had used Peter's Christian name as well as the fact that he had, apparently, been helping her to get organised. But strangely, I couldn't feel jealous. I had liked her when I first met her and now her friendliness and her pleasant smile struck me as completely natural and guileless. It had been a long while since I had had a girl of my own age to talk to and I found myself relaxing as she busied herself making coffee for us. She did most of the talking and was obviously intrigued by the present situation in which she found herself.

'I don't often nurse murder victims!' she said as she finally sat down opposite me, pushing the little white nurse's cap further back on her black hair. 'Thank goodness, though, I don't think my patient is going to die. Dr Farran seems very pleased with her.

Incredible old girl, isn't she?'

We talked for a few moments of Lady Barclay and then Angela returned to the subject of the poison.

'The police were here early this morning searching everywhere,' she told me confidentially. 'Don't know what they were looking for but they went off with a box of peppermint creams. Do you suppose there might be arsenic in them?'

I shook my head, explaining that Lady Barclay had a weakness for peppermint creams and had a standing order with a London store to send her a box every second week. She kept them in the top drawer of her escritoire.

Angela nodded.

'Yes, that's where they found them. I just can't fathom who would want to harm the old lady. She seems such a dear! Peter said the only person in the household with a motive was the American, but he seems nice, too.'

'Peter had no right to cast suspicions on anyone,' I said crossly. 'He only arrived in England yesterday so he can't possibly know what's been going on. He should mind his own business.'

Angela gave me a long, searching look

over the rim of her coffee cup.

'Forgive me for asking, Jenny, but are you two actually engaged to be married? I know it isn't any of my business but … well, you aren't wearing a ring and…'

'I'd really rather not discuss it!' I broke in. As Angela herself had said, it *was* none of her business. She didn't seem in the least put out by my curt rebuff. She chattered on innocently, saying:

'I think your Peter is fabulous – so well mannered and yet lots of fun, too. I envy you, Jenny. I never seem to meet nice guys who are handsome as well. They are either good looking and not nice or vice versa. I've only been in love once – with a fellow a bit like your Peter, except he was married and just playing around. Just my luck to find myself attracted to another one who's bespoke!'

I found Angela's remark profoundly disturbing. She was being frank to the point of embarrassing me, telling me in so many words that, if it weren't for me, she'd be seriously interested in Peter. Perhaps, if it weren't for me, Peter might be seriously interested in Angela? He seemed to have spent a remarkable lot of time in her company since yesterday!

'Anyway, I'm glad he isn't going back to London today after all,' Angela went on unaware of the effect her remarks were having on me. 'It's nice having young people around the place. Sometimes nursing old people can be terribly depressing without the breath of life to ease the atmosphere of approaching death.'

I had not known that Peter had decided to stay on. But then, since I had not seen him since breakfast, I suppose he had not had a chance to tell me.

'Did Peter tell you why he was staying?' I found myself asking.

'But of course – because the police said he must.' Angela sounded surprised. 'Didn't he tell you? Everyone has to stick around until the mystery is cleared up … a sort of house arrest, I suppose.'

I stood up, thanked Angela for the coffee and went while the impulse was still strong, in search of Peter.

He was in the garden, sitting under the beech tree reading the morning paper. Seeing me coming he jumped up looking I thought, a little guilty. It crossed my mind, as perhaps it did his, that *he* had not come in search of *me*.

I sat down beside him and told him I'd

been having a chat with Angela. I thanked him for making himself useful to her. Peter gave me a quizzical glance which I ignored.

'You're not jealous, are you?' he asked.

'What gave you that idea?' I asked calmly.

'Well, you sounded a bit sarcastic – as if you thought I ought not to have helped Angela or something!'

'Don't be childish!' I said crossly. 'Why shouldn't you help her? And why should I be jealous? Ought I to be?'

The question hung in the air between us. Peter broke the silence eventually, saying:

'Well, if you really cared about me, you might have objected. After all, she is a very pretty girl!'

'Were you trying to make me jealous, then?' I asked stiffly.

'Of course not!' Peter retorted crossly. 'But maybe I should now you've suggested it. You can't say you've shown me much warmth since I came back.'

He sounded aggrieved and, in a moment of self-truth, I had to admit he was justified. I had been pretty stand-offish. But then I hadn't felt like flinging myself into his arms – not after the way he'd treated me in the past. I hoped his pride was hurt – as he had hurt mine.

Quite suddenly I found that I was hating myself. I had discovered an insufferable vindictiveness in my nature that I didn't like one bit. I had subconsciously been out to hurt Peter because I'd been hurt. It wasn't very nice to say the least.

'I'm sorry!' I said genuinely. 'I suppose it's proving harder than I expected to ... to forgive you.'

'Forgive me?' Peter sounded surprised. 'You mean because of Christine?'

'No,' I replied truthfully. 'Because of the way you walked out and left me. I was desperately in love with you then, Peter, and it hurt like hell. I couldn't have left you.'

'Oh, that!' Peter said, dismissing it as of no consequence. 'But you knew why I went, Jenny. We needed the money.'

'You needed it!' I said. 'I wanted to get married. We had the cottage all ready and we could have managed it. You didn't have to go.'

Peter was frowning, as if this aspect had only just occurred to him.

'I suppose not!' he admitted. 'Though at the time I felt I was doing the right thing – for both of us.'

'Maybe you did at that!' I said thoughtfully. 'Maybe our engagement had gone on too long and we were right to separate when we did. We both found that we could get along without each other, didn't we? It tested us – and found us both wanting.'

Peter's face was white beneath the tan.

'Are you telling me you don't want to marry after all?' he asked. 'That you've found out you aren't in love with me any more?'

'I don't know. Perhaps I am!' I was surprised to hear my own words. 'Are you sure you are in love with me, Peter? Maybe we are both trying to stir up dead embers, without much success. There's a saying, isn't there, that nothing is as dead as a dead love.'

I waited for Peter to argue, to convince me that I was talking nonsense. But he stayed silent and suddenly I knew what was wrong between us – had been wrong ever since his return ... we had quite simply fallen out of love with each other. We'd grown apart during the months of our separation and no matter how much we might both want it otherwise, we weren't going to grow close to each other again.

'I've made a real mess of things, haven't I?' Peter said gloomily. 'I suppose all the time I'd been imagining you were still in love with me, you were falling for someone else.'

'There's no one else!' I was shouting and with an effort I lowered my voice. 'I mean, I'm not in love with anyone – you or anyone. Okay?'

'I don't know what to say – except that I'm sorry!' Peter said. 'I suppose this is no more than I deserve.'

'Oh, don't be silly, Peter!' I told him. 'It's not really anybody's fault. Admit that you aren't even mildly heartbroken. You don't love me the way people ought to love when they get married. It's your pride, not your heart, that's damaged.'

'How can you say that, Jenny?' Peter said reproachfully.

'Because it's true!' I told him with new conviction. 'Let's call it a day, Peter, before we let ourselves get caught up again in something we don't either of us really want.'

I was almost as surprised as Peter to hear myself talking this way. But I knew without any doubt that I was right. I didn't love him. I'd been in love with the idea of loving him. His homecoming had failed to arouse me to any of the former feeling I'd had for him. Now I could only feel dispassionate and I was convinced that that was how he felt for me.

He protested for a little while – but without much heart behind his protestations. Finally he admitted that our reunion had fallen a little flat for him too, and not only because of the coolness of my behaviour.

'Now I'm back in England, I'd hate to think I'd never see you, Jenny. Do we have to make a complete break?'

'Why should we?' I asked, suddenly at peace with him and strangely happy. 'We don't have to follow the conventional dramatic ending, do we? I'd like to stay friends – if you would.'

He reached out a hand and took mine. Just for a moment I wondered if after all I had been wrong and the affection I still felt for him might not deepen once more, when life was more normal again, into love. But the doubt was transitory and I saw that instant of intimacy for what it really was – a sentimental invocation of the past. I wouldn't let it confuse the present again.

'You're quite sure that this is the way you want it, Jenny?'

I nodded, gently withdrawing my hand from his.

'Yes, I'm sure,' I said.

Then I saw Allan walking towards us, waving his arm as if he had something urgent to tell us. I felt my heartbeat quicken and once again an extraordinary clarity left my mind achingly aware of the truth. In the same way that I had suddenly discovered I did not love Peter, so had I suddenly discovered the reason why. I was in love with Allan.

I had no time to grasp fully the importance of the realisation for Allan was calling to us to come back to the house as quickly as possible.

'Lord Barclay wants us all to join him in the library,' he said. 'There have been some important developments and the police now know who it was who attempted to kill the old lady.'

I shivered with a sudden nameless fear. Ignoring Peter, just as if he were not there at all, Allan came over and put his arm round my shoulder.

'Don't be too upset, Jenny,' he said softly. 'But I'm afraid it was Simon.'

I gasped, shocked into silence. It was too horrible to take in – yet I knew Allan would not have told me unless it were true.

'So the peppermint creams weren't poisoned after all?'

'Yes, they were. Simon sent them to Lady Barclay and she mistook them for her regular order which is what he hoped would happen.

You know how absent minded she can be when her thoughts are concentrated on her book. Well, the parcel arrived midmorning and was taken to her study by the servant with Lady Barclay's elevenses. She never thought to look closely at the wrapping or postmark. The police found them and that's how they traced the deed back to Simon.'

'It's … unbelievable!' I whispered.

'Don't be too upset!' Allan said again. 'The important thing to remember, darling, is that Simon's plan didn't succeed. Lady Barclay is going to be all right. That's what counts, isn't it!'

I hung on to this thought during the nightmare hour that followed, comforted by it as Allan had known I would be; and comforted even more by the endearment he had used so naturally but so meaningfully to me.

14

Already the leaves of the great beech tree were turning to red and gold. There was still warmth in the soft September sunshine but I had tucked a rug round Lady Barclay's frail little body just to be on the safe side. Although she had long since recovered from the dreadful attempt to poison her, she had never quite regained her old health and vigour. I did not want to think that perhaps Allan was right and she was very slowly failing; that maybe she would not live to see another Spring. Yet as I sat beside her, the day before my wedding, it seemed as if she wanted to talk about death though I had tried several times to steer her away from the subject.

'Jenny dear, death holds no fears for me,' she said. 'I have done everything I wanted to do and I'm quite ready now when the time comes. I'm afraid of only one thing – that you will grieve for me.'

Tears stung the back of my eyes.

'Please don't!' I whispered.

She put her small hand, almost transparent it seemed to me, over mine and patted it gently.

'You are on the threshold of a new life, child. It would be very wrong of you to let the past mar the happiness I know is coming to you. If you could only realise how happy I am, too! My book finished at last! My life's work completed and with such a happy ending. I feel that the dear Lord must have lent a guiding hand to Allan, bringing him to us all the way from America just when we both needed him so much.'

I lay back on the grass, my hands supporting my head and stared up into the branches of the great tree. It was hundreds of years old – probably stood here in the days when Clarissa Barclay had eloped to Canada with young Edwin Howe. It was part of the family in a way – part of a family which tomorrow I, too, would join.

I thought of the quiet wedding Allan and I were having in the village church next day. Lady Barclay would be there in the family pew, determined as she had been from the first, to be well enough to attend. Allan said he thought she was clinging to life for just two reasons – to see *The Crimson Tapestry* in print and to see us married!

'She'll be here when we get back from our honeymoon,' he kept telling me. 'After all, darling, the book isn't being published until Christmas and she'll hang on till then, you see!'

I hoped he was right. We were going to America for our honeymoon and Allan would settle his affairs over there and return here to take over the management of the estate under Lord Barclay's guidance. He'd promised Lady Barclay that he would take up his rightful place in the house and would not even discuss with me whether he really wished to do this. He'd once said his roots were in America but he would not let me remind him of it. Instead, he reminded me that he'd also said he could be tempted to stay if he had the right wife and children and now he had me he had no regrets.

I loved Allan for many reasons. His loving kindness and tenderness with Lady Barclay was not the least of them. I loved him also for the complete lack of jealousy he'd shown towards Peter who had spent a good deal of time at the Manor ever since that dreadful week following Lady Barclay's illness. Of course Allan knew as well as I did that Angela and not I was the bait which brought Peter down most weekends. Nevertheless, we had become very good friends and if anyone at all was jealous, it was I of the way the two men seemed to get on so well. Peter and Angela would both be in church tomorrow. Lord Barclay was coming, too, of course, and strangely enough, Julia.

It was strange, I mused, how Simon's death had brought Julia so much closer to her husband. The terrible tragedy which Allan kept insisting was a blessing in disguise, had brought about a complete nervous collapse and Julia had spent two months in a psychiatric ward. When she emerged Lord Barclay brought her home, a rather pathetic, subdued, dependent Julia who never spoke of the son she had so adored and clung to her husband as if he and not Simon had been the love of her life.

I tried not to think too often of Simon. He was obviously mentally unbalanced from the start. At the time he had been found to have sent Lady Barclay the poisoned peppermints, Julia had confessed that he had had some insane idea that Lady Barclay was trying to get at him; first by persuading me to have nothing to do with him and also by bringing Allan into the house to supplant him. In actual fact, Lady Barclay had always felt rather sorry for Simon, even while she disliked and distrusted him. Certainly, my rejection of him had not been caused by her but because of his own behaviour with drugs.

The police never did catch up with him. He killed himself in a car accident on the M1 before they could even accuse him of attempted murder. So there was no trial, no case and no further blot on the family name. In fact, no one really suffered except poor Julia who had tried for so many years to protect and shield him, knowing all the time that she was fighting a losing battle. At least now, for her, the battle was over. She was rather pathetic and Allan and I had been very touched to see how gentle and kind and protective Lord Barclay was to her, especially in view of the way she had treated him for so many years. They had both moved down to live permanently at the Manor House whilst Allan and I were away so that they could jointly take care of Lady Barclay. I was glad she would have someone here. Angela was leaving at the end of the month and the old lady still needed someone to take care of her.

I was fairly sure that before very long Angela and Peter would be following Allan's and my example and getting married. I knew Angela was genuinely in love with Peter for she had told me so often enough. But Peter seemed in no hurry to settle down.

'I expect he will, once you're tied to me!' Allan said laughing. 'I think he's still just a little bit in love with you, darling!'

Lady Barclay broke in on my thoughts.

'With that look on your face, child, you must be thinking of your young man!' she said with her usual astuteness. 'You have the most transparent face, Jenny!'

I sat up, smiling.

'I could tell a lie and say you were wrong!'

'You love him very much, don't you?' she said gently.

'More than I thought it possible ever to love anyone,' I replied. 'It's strange, really – at first I liked him, then I thought I disliked him, then for a long while I was irritated by him – and all the time I was just fighting the truth – that I loved him. Oh, Lady Barclay, suppose he'd been less patient and under- standing! Suppose he'd not waited for me to grow up! Suppose he'd never fallen in love with me! Suppose he'd never even come to England at all!'

'And suppose pigs could fly!' said my dear old lady. 'I told you, Jenny, it was all Fated. After all, suppose you'd never come to help me write *The Crimson Tapestry*.'

'You'd still have met Allan even if I hadn't. You'd still have had that last chapter to your book!' I reminded her.

The faded blue eyes looked back into mine with a twinkle.

'Perhaps,' she said. 'But I could not have ended it like any good fairy tale, could I? Now I've been able to say "So they lived happily ever after!"'

'That's foretelling the future, not the past,' I said.

But I had no doubt at all in my mind that she would be proved right.

The publishers hope that this book has given you enjoyable reading. Large Print Books are especially designed to be as easy to see and hold as possible. If you wish a complete list of our books please ask at your local library or write directly to:

Dales Large Print Books
Magna House, Long Preston,
Skipton, North Yorkshire.
BD23 4ND

This Large Print Book, for people
who cannot read normal print,
is published under the auspices of

THE ULVERSCROFT FOUNDATION